IRONTON SEP 200
STE. GENEVIEVE MA
STEELVILLE
BOURBON

FREDERICKTOWN JAN 200

F
DAR   Dark, Sandra
           Calypso wind.

$15.95

	DATE DUE	

OZARK REGIONAL LIBRARY
HEADQUARTERS, IRONTON

CALYPSO WIND

Other books by Sandra Dark:

Silent Cathedrals

CALYPSO WIND

•

Sandra Dark

AVALON BOOKS
NEW YORK

© Copyright 2006 by Sandra Dark
All rights reserved.
All the characters in this book are fictitious,
and any resemblance to actual persons,
living or dead, is purely coincidental.
Published by Thomas Bouregy & Co., Inc.
160 Madison Avenue, New York, NY 10016

Library of Congress Cataloging-in-Publication Data

Dark, Sandra.
Calypso wind / Sandra Dark.
p. cm.
Novel.
ISBN 0-8034-9775-X (hardcover : acid-free paper)
I. Title.

PS3604.A753C35 2006
813'.6—dc22
2005035235

PRINTED IN THE UNITED STATES OF AMERICA
ON ACID-FREE PAPER
BY HADDON CRAFTSMEN, BLOOMSBURG, PENNSYLVANIA

To Peggy Lovret Chaffin,
whose heart is a work of art.

Chapter One

A herring gull swept gracefully past the tenth floor office window, scudding along beneath dull winter clouds. As attorney Ben Ross watched the seabird bank sharply toward Boston Harbor, the bleak sky seemed to reflect his mood.

Price Carmichael had been more than his boss. Price had been his father figure, his mentor, his idol. And now he was gone.

Ben slumped into his desk chair, flipped open a leather-bound folder, and stared at the cashier's check made out to Price's long-lost niece. Price would have called the check a velvet-lined trap. Ben figured no trap would be necessary. After all, who wouldn't leap at a chance to inherit the Carmichael fortune, thanks to an accident of birth?

Distracted, he leafed through the meager file on Carrie Washburn. She would be twenty-two now, but the only photo the private investigator that Ben had hired had come up with was a high school yearbook image of a rather gawky teen. Even with braces and pixie-short wheat-colored hair, she had been borderline cute back then. From the slight downward tilt of her head, Ben pegged her as shy. But a lot could change in four years.

The investigator had finally tracked her down in Atlanta, where she seemed to live pretty much hand-to-mouth, attending college part-time and working for a company called Galaxy Tours. By the time Ben caught up with her tomorrow, she would be playing tour guide to a bunch of tourists in Jamaica.

Ben sighed. Just finding Carrie Washburn had taken nearly three months. That left the deadline for getting her to agree to the conditions of her uncle's will barely a week away. As if she would require much persuasion.

Carrying out the will was the last thing he could do for Price. So, even though handing over the Carmichael fortune to Price's niece would end Ben's long and cherished relationship with the old man, he was ready to get it over with.

The office door bumped open. Ben swiveled sideways as Edmund barged in, tore around the desk and lunged onto his lap.

"Bad dog, Eddie," he murmured, gently stroking the black Labrador's broad head.

"Mr. Ross, he'll ruin your suit!" Edna Kincade

appeared in the doorway, shaking her head. "I'll never understand why Mr. Carmichael insisted on having that lummox around the office."

Ben eased the hundred and ten pound load off his lap and brushed at his pinstriped suit. "Price enjoyed showing him off, Edna. He paid a wad for Eddie's classy pedigree."

"Pedigree?" The gray-haired secretary made a disparaging sound, but eyed the dog with affection. "Speaking of his heritage—since you appear to have inherited Edmund, do you wish to continue having his chest dyed?"

Ben gave her a blank look.

"The white spot on his chest," she added. Her eyes widened behind her round glasses. "I thought you knew."

He rested a hand on Eddie's head, confused. "Edna, purebred Labs don't have white spots. Anywhere."

"Precisely." Arching a brow at Ben, she adjusted the jacket of her designer suit, then patted her substantial thigh. "Come along, Edmund."

The dog loped out of the room, wagging.

When the door closed, Ben sat frowning for a long moment. He couldn't imagine why Price hadn't sent Edmund back to the breeder when he discovered the flaw. It wasn't like the old man to tolerate imperfection of any kind, let alone pay through the nose for it.

For some reason, that train of thought led Ben straight back to Carrie Washburn. He picked up the photo and stared at Price's only living relative—the one Price had never breathed a word about. Cute... braces or no braces, she was definitely cute. And by month's end, the mysterious Miss Washburn would be rich beyond her wildest dreams.

And you, Ross old pal, will be out in the cold.

But duty called.

Ben slid the folder into the briefcase that held his plane ticket, and headed for the airport.

With a whoosh of air brakes, the bus turned onto the long driveway leading into the Calypso Beach Resort. Seated next to her boss on the front row, Carrie took a nervous peek back at the first group that Galaxy Tours had brought to Calypso Beach since being put on probation by the resort.

Clients in gaudy tropical shirts and straw hats chattered among themselves. Some snapped pictures out the windows.

Lana Fuller elbowed her. "Relax, sugar," she murmured. "It'll be fine."

Carrie watched Lana produce a silver compact from her fishnet purse, casually check her flawless makeup, and pat her long, raven hair. The woman didn't look the least bit concerned. Carrie wished she could say the same for herself.

The posh Jamaican resort had suffered a rash of room burglaries during Galaxy's previous visit earlier in the month. Management had served notice that if

Calypso Wind

history repeated itself during this stay, Galaxy Tours would be permanently banned from Calypso Beach. That would destroy Lana's business reputation.

But the disaster wouldn't end there. Carrie would lose her tour guide job—along with any hope of affording her next semester of college back in Atlanta.

A tanned face appeared over the top of the seat's headrest. "I can't get enough of this scenery."

Carrie smiled back at Mark Hanes. "Apparently not."

The earlier, burglary-plagued visit to Calypso Beach had been part of a ten-day, six-island excursion. The Cleveland accountant was among the members of that tour who had chosen to return for an extended two-week stay at the resort. Unlike Mark, most of the others in the tour group were retirees.

Mark gave a self-conscious laugh. He had a slight cleft in his chin that Carrie had found attractive on first sight. But the sharp contrast between his white-blond hair and deep, swimming-pool tan made her suspect that either his hair color or his tan had come from a bottle.

He cleared his throat and leaned a little closer.

Carrie tensed, sensing what was to come. On the earlier trip, Mark seemed to have developed a crush on her. She sometimes found his persistent attentions embarrassing, but she didn't want to seem rude.

"Are you busy this evening?" he asked.

For once, Carrie was prepared.

"No, Mark, but you will be. Have you lost your copy

of the tour schedule?" She dug a glossy four-color brochure from her tote bag. "Tonight you'll all be savoring jerk chicken on the beach while limbo dancing to the reggae beat of a steel-drum band."

Mark's smile took a slight downturn. But he accepted the schedule and settled back in his seat, trying to look intrigued.

Catching Lana's expression, Carrie murmured, "What are you smirking at?"

Lana nodded toward the seat behind them and mouthed, "Easy pickings."

Lana had an outrageous ten-point rating system for men that ranged from "Pushover" up to "Impossible Dream." "Easy Pickings" ranked next to the bottom. Carrie blushed, as her boss had known she would.

"By the way," Lana said, "can you chaperone tomorrow night? I have a date with a pilot."

Her business is on the ropes, and she just can't stop partying, Carrie thought. But she nodded, as Lana had known she would.

"Oh, Arnie, isn't that just the most gorgeous thing you've ever seen in all your born days?"

Clutching a ball of chartreuse crochet yarn to her buxom chest, Sybil Rodgers paused in the second floor hallway as a waiter carried a large, cellophane-wrapped basket of tropical fruits into her room.

Arnold Rodgers patted his ample belly and chuckled at his wife. "Dibs on the papaya, sweetheart."

Calypso Wind 7

The retired insurance salesman from Chicago was wearing yet another toupee, Carrie noted. This was the fourth Caribbean trip the Rodgers had taken with Galaxy Tours, and Sybil's husband had sported a different hairpiece each time. The current edition appeared to have been scalped from Ted Koppel.

Carrie waited until they followed the waiter into their room, then continued along the slate-tiled hallway. Turning a corner, she rechecked the pink message slip the desk clerk had handed her. *J. Benjamin Ross.* The name didn't ring a bell, but J. Benjamin must know her, because the message said he wished to speak with her ASAP.

She was intrigued, to say the least. No one other than tour clients had ever left a message for her. Since his room was one floor below hers, she had decided to swing by on her way up, to salve her curiosity.

As it turned out, she found the correct room number on a gold-trimmed beige door that signified a luxury suite.

So, she thought, J. Benjamin has bucks.

Carrie rapped lightly on the door.

And waited.

She knocked again, a bit louder. This time, a muffled response came from within. A long moment later, the lock clicked and the door swung open.

"I told you to use—" The husky voice shut off abruptly.

Carrie was studying a worn strap on her sandal when

the door opened. The first thing she saw was a pair of mirror-polished black wingtip shoes beneath crisp pinstriped cuffs. Her gaze drifted up past a snow-white T-shirt to a broad shelf of towel-draped shoulders. A hand clutched the towel—and also in that hand, a gleaming straight razor.

Carrie stared at a thin ribbon of soap on the long blade, thinking how wonderfully the old-fashioned shaving tool went with the wingtips. The owner suddenly vanished.

"Come on in." The husky baritone rumbled from deep inside the suite, carrying a regional accent that Carrie couldn't quite place.

She eased cautiously inside, leaving the door open.

The spacious sitting room was furnished with bright floral chairs and marble-top tables—quite a contrast to Carrie's dinky economy class accommodations on the third floor. Across the room, a balmy sea breeze billowed sheer curtains over the doorway to a wide balcony, filtering a breathtaking view of the sea. A cacophony of distant voices peppered the rhythmic thud of surf rolling onto immaculate sand.

"Sorry for the way I answered the door," he called from beyond a door to the left. "I thought you were room service."

Seconds later, the man ducked back into the sitting room. He had put on a crisp blue shirt, and was pegging gold-and-onyx links into the cuffs.

Carrie took her first real look at his angular features

and lean, freshly shaved jaw. Stylishly razor-cut chocolate hair tousled across a wide forehead. He had the fit and trim body of a male model and, judging by his clothes—not to mention the luxury suite—a champagne-and-caviar bank account to go with it. But it was his eyes that captivated Carrie—ordinary hazel on the surface, they were imbedded with coppery chips, like tiny glowing cinders.

For a discomforting moment, he simply stared at her, his head cocked as if taking her measure. Carrie had never felt so—inspected.

At last remembering what had brought her there, she held up the message slip. "Are . . . uhm . . . are you J. Benjamin Ross?"

"Ben . . . please. And you're Miss Washburn?"

She nodded. After another pause, she waved the message slip and asked, "Do I get a clue?" Carrie's voice betrayed growing tension. The way he kept staring at her made her edgy.

He gave her a questioning look.

"Are you selling something?" she asked. Tired from the long flight down from Atlanta, she wanted to get on to her own room and shower off the fatigue.

"Selling?" Ben burst out laughing.

He had a good laugh that dramatically altered his features and revealed a slight space between his strong front teeth. When he regained his composure, Carrie found that she missed the wry, Huckleberry Finn grin. She had found it somewhat endearing.

"May I call you Caroline?" he asked.

"Carrie," she said automatically, then wished she hadn't granted the informality to a stranger.

Ben seemed to catch the shift in her expression and smiled again, as if trying to reassure her. It did a little. He had an expressive face, she noted.

"May I ask you a few personal questions, Carrie?"

"Uhm . . . I don't think so."

Ben studied his shoes and appeared to regroup. "Not intimate questions, Carrie. I just need to make sure I'm talking to the right Caroline Washburn."

Nervous though she was, Carrie was too curious not to nod.

"Your full name is Caroline Marie Washburn?"

"Yes."

"Your mother's given name was Marie Elena?"

"Yes."

"You grew up in Philadelphia?"

Nod.

"Moved to Atlanta after high school, and enrolled at Georgia Tech on a hardship scholarship?"

"Partial scholarship. I'm mostly working my way through."

"You're on track to get a four-year degree in—what?—six years?"

She kept bobbing her head, wondering where he had dug up all this information on her. And why. "Look, are you with some kind of collection agency? Because my student loans aren't due until—"

Calypso Wind 11

"No, no." He threw up both hands.

His boyish smile kept her from bolting. "Then why this invasion of my privacy?"

"I'm an attorney, Carrie." He seemed to be choosing his words. "From Boston."

"Oh?" That explained the accent. But J. Benjamin Ross didn't fit Carrie's image of a stuffy Boston lawyer—not with that homespun smile.

"I represent Price Carmichael."

Carrie froze. For an endless moment, her lungs refused to take in air. Slowly, she took a step back toward the hallway door. When she finally found her voice, she said, "Then we have nothing to discuss, Mr. Ross."

"Ben . . . call me Ben." A small frown line appeared between his eyes. "I'm executor of your uncle's will."

She blinked, startled by the news that her uncle had died. Carrie waited for the emotion to hit, but she was too numb. In a daze, she turned to leave.

"Wait, Carrie. Please. We have to talk about this."

"No. Absolutely not."

Ben's expression showed that this was not the reaction he had expected. He came toward her, cautiously, as if approaching a skittish cat. When they were close enough, he reached out a hand, not quite touching her arm.

"You don't understand," he said. "Your Uncle Price has passed away."

"I got that."

"You're his only surviving blood relative."

"I know."

"You're his heir."

"Absolutely not," she repeated.

He looked stunned.

Once again, she moved to leave.

"Please . . . wait." This time he did touch her, barely brushing her arm with his fingertips.

His gentleness made her skin tingle.

He drew his hand away quickly and shoved it into his pocket. Pawing at his hair, he glanced around as if scrambling for a thought.

"Okay," he said. "Let's do this. Give me one hour of your time in the restaurant of your choice." He seemed to hold his breath, waiting. Then, softly, once again, "Please."

Carrie took a deep, steadying breath. When the attorney touched her a moment ago, she had suddenly, inexplicably, lost her urge to take flight. One fleeting touch and she unaccountably felt at ease with J. Benjamin Ross.

No, it's his smile, she decided. *He has what Mom used to call a big-hearted smile . . . when it's there.*

But they were talking about Price Carmichael, and the idea of sitting down to dinner with the shadow of her uncle didn't appeal to Carrie one little bit.

In the interest of getting this conversation over and done with, she resigned herself to giving the lawyer five more minutes of her time. She didn't want to be rude.

"Why can't you just tell me what you have to right now?" she asked.

"That was my intention." Ben glanced over his shoulder at an expensive leather attaché case on the dresser. He seemed bewildered. His disarming smile returned, looking strained. "But now, something tells me it might be better if we did this on neutral territory."

Torn between her attraction to Ben's smile and her equally intense aversion to his mission, Carrie rubbed both arms. "Mr. Ross, you're making me itch."

He shrugged helplessly and spread both hands, as if he knew the feeling. The smile tilted.

"Tell me," he said, "if I got down on my knees and begged, would you find the gesture pathetic or persuasive?"

She smiled back in spite of herself. As much as she wanted to flee the very name of Price Carmichael—as she had every reason to—she didn't feel the same about her uncle's lawyer. Carrie was seldom wrong about people, and found that her instincts were setting off no alarms at all about Ben Ross.

To her astonishment, he started to lower himself to one knee.

"All right, all right," she blurted with a nervous laugh. "One hour."

He straightened, exhaling in exaggerated relief. "You're a hard sell, Carrie."

"I thought you said you weren't selling anything."

He shook his head. "Well, I sure wasn't planning on having to, that's for sure."

Ben followed her out of the suite.

A young couple in bathing suits came toward them down the hallway, headed in the direction of the elevator bank. Ahead of them romped a toddler carrying a red beach ball. As they drew near, the tot suddenly dropped the ball and made a beeline for Ben, throwing her pudgy arms around his leg.

"How about eight-thirty?" Ben asked Carrie.

"That works." She watched, bemused, as he leaned over and gently pried the tyke loose with hardly a downward glance, as if strange babies clinging to his legs were a common occurrence. "Let me know where to meet you," she added.

"I'll pick you up."

Carrie hesitated, then made up her mind that she wasn't ready to cede that much control to Ben Ross. She shook her head and repeated, "Call and let me know where to meet you. I'll get there on my own, thanks."

As the parents rushed to retrieve their toddler, Carrie took the opportunity to leave, wondering if she had just made a serious mistake.

Waving off the couple's apologies, Ben glanced up the hallway in time to glimpse Carrie disappearing around the corner. Since high school, her hair had darkened to a deep honey color, cascading in luxuriant waves down past her shoulder blades. She had shed the gawkiness of adolescence along with the braces, maturing into an attractive young woman.

Admit it, Ross—she's a full-fledged knockout even if she doesn't seem to realize it. And she makes you nervous as all get-out.

He rubbed the back of his neck. Carrie's reaction to the mere mention of Price Carmichael had blindsided him. Ben had expected a show of interest, perhaps even a spark of outright greed. After all, the private investigator's report had left no doubt that Carrie Washburn was poor as a church mouse. Instead, she hadn't just turned cold to the news of potential riches, she had physically backed away. He'd had to scramble just to get her to agree to another meeting.

Shaking his head, Ben stepped back into his suite. For the sake of order, he tried to put a label on Carrie Washburn. The only word that came to mind was *innocent*. But he knew she had to be stronger and more complex than that. In this day and age, to work your way through college while supporting yourself required a determination that bordered on stubbornness.

Innocence and determination. He found that combination both refreshing and appealing.

For perhaps the thousandth time in the past three months, Ben wondered why Price Carmichael had never mentioned having a niece, let alone a sister. The inexplicable omission troubled him. For more than a dozen years, Ben had been as close to the old man as a son—or so he had thought. Having been left out of the loop was hard to accept.

With effort, Ben shoved that thought from his mind. He had a lot to do before eight-thirty.

Chapter Two

On a wooden perch near the door, a large black cockatoo raised its crest of feathers and let out an ear-splitting screech. Ben executed a crisp about-face and resumed pacing in the opposite direction, weaving through the dense crowd in the lobby of the Sand Dollar Restaurant. Every time he got near the bird, it screamed and extended a scaly foot toward his shoulder. The thing was beginning to get on his nerves.

He checked his watch again. Carrie Washburn was ten minutes late. Not a good sign.

His hand moved to the thick sheaf of papers in the inside pocket of his tropical-blue sports coat. He hadn't been this wound up since the week he took his bar exam.

Ben pivoted at the far end of the lobby, and had

almost made it back to the Budgie from Hell when the outside door opened. He glimpsed dark honey hair as Carrie stood on tiptoe, trying to scan the crowd. As he moved toward her, she spotted him and produced what he classed as a starter-smile. Ben smiled back, noticing how her skin glowed in the muted lighting.

"Sorry I'm late," she said. "Mark Ha—one of the tour clients waylaid me as I was leaving Calypso Beach."

She seemed slightly out of breath, as if she had run all the way up the beach from the resort. Ben realized that, on Carrie's budget, she probably had done just that. He kicked himself for not having arranged for her transportation.

"It was worth the wait, Carrie."

He held out a hand, and was surprised by a rush of pure pleasure when she accepted it. The twisted spaghetti straps of her hibiscus-flowered cotton dress left her shoulders bare. She wore only a hint of make-up, and no jewelry. In his opinion, she needed neither.

Ben tucked her hand into the crook of his arm as Carrie walked stiffly beside him, a steady reminder that she was a reluctant guest.

They crossed an arched wooden bridge over one of several fish tanks sunken into the floor of the sprawling restaurant. Designed to mimic miniature ponds, the tanks were connected by meandering streams. Bamboo railings ran alongside the waterways, serving as perch highways for a colorful assortment of tame birds.

"Aren't we supposed to wait to be seated?" Carrie asked as Ben steered her around an outcropping of lush greenery.

"I've reserved a quiet table where we can talk."

Beyond the tubbed plants, they stepped onto a raised platform nearly filled by a glass-and-bamboo table and two cushioned chairs. Sliding glass doors had been pulled back, presenting an open-air view of the moonlit beach beyond an apron of wooden decking.

"Lovely," Carrie murmured, taking in the secluded setting as Ben held a chair out for her. "I really had no idea. . . ."

"You've never eaten here?"

She laughed nervously. "On my meal allowance? Not likely."

Pleased that the Sand Dollar was something special to her, Ben settled into the chair across from her. Carrie fingered the rim of a cut-glass bowl with three floating candles at the center of the table. When she looked up, her eyes widened slightly. He turned around to see what had attracted her attention.

A small green parrot with a red head had sidled along the railing, taking up position less than a foot from Ben's shoulder. The bird began preening itself as a waiter appeared with two umbrella-garnished drinks on a wooden tray.

"I took the liberty of ordering ahead," Ben said. "I hope you don't mind."

Carrie shook her head. She quietly accepted her Mai

Tai, setting it aside as she turned her head to gaze out at the beach.

Ah, Carrie Washburn doesn't drink, Ben noted, mentally filing that away. He set his own drink aside. While her attention was on the surf hissing onto the beach, he could drink her in instead, without being impolite.

At the time he had bribed the maitre d' into reserving the Sand Dollar's most private table on short notice, Ben hadn't realized the cozy alcove would feel so—romantic. He wondered if Carrie thought so, too, or if it just struck him that way because he had a better view.

The daytime sea breeze had died down. Soon a warm night breeze would spring up, blowing off the island out to sea. But for now, he could detect the faint floral scent of Carrie's perfume hovering in the still air. Everything about her was as tantalizing and subtle as a slow sunrise.

Ben frowned to himself. He had come to Jamaica on a mission. But when he was around Carrie Washburn, he had trouble keeping his mind on the topic at hand.

"Have you ever been to Jamaica before?" she asked, resting her chin on her hand.

Carrie had a direct way of looking at him that was almost as distracting as the candlelight dancing in her eyes.

"Many times," he said. "Some close friends have a place near Half Moon Bay."

She arched a brow. "They don't let you stay there?"

"Actually, they built on a room for me."

Calypso Wind 21

The other brow went up. "But you're staying at Calypso Beach. Was there a problem with your room?"

He grinned and, without thinking, reached across the table to touch her hand. "They don't know I'm here, Carrie. I flew down to meet with you exclusively."

She withdrew her hand, suddenly looking uncertain and guarded.

Ben quickly leaned back, giving her more space. He hadn't meant to touch her—his hand seemed to have drifted across the table of its own accord. Now it went just as reflexively to the sheaf of papers in his coat pocket.

He warned himself to move cautiously. If he had learned one thing from trout fishing with Price Carmichael, it was the value of patience. Besides, just sitting there with Carrie gave him an unfamiliar sense of peace. He was in no hurry to break that bubble.

Carrie had returned her gaze to the beach, though a tiny frown line between her eyes indicated that her thoughts had turned inward. The waiter broke the long silence by bringing salads dripping with fruit dressing. As Carrie shifted her attention back to the table, she glanced at Ben—and her expression lit up with wonder. Realizing that she was looking past him again, he turned to check on the little hookbill.

A white cockatoo had joined the small green-and-red parrot, along with a blue macaw and a long-necked gray parrot with a too-small head. The smaller parrots fluffed their feathers and yawned elaborately in each other's faces, jockeying for position on the railing. With graceful aplomb, the macaw leaned over and grasped the lapel of Ben's sports coat with its huge beak, cocking its head to look up at him, its pupils alternately dilating and pinpricking.

Clamping a protective hand over the papers in his inside pocket, Ben pried the beak off his lapel, and turned back to face Carrie.

She smiled with delight. "Where did they all come from?"

He shrugged. "South America, Africa . . . maybe Australia."

"No, I mean . . ." Carrie watched a small bright-yellow hookbill come scurrying along the railing from the main dining room. "Oh, never mind."

The way she kept gazing out at the beach made Ben suspect that she was trying to avoid looking at him. Then he noticed that she was staring at his dim reflection in the glass of the retracted door. Suddenly self-conscious, he reached up to straighten his tie before remembering that he wasn't wearing one.

They ate quietly. Between courses, they made polite conversation, Carrie drawing on a seemingly limitless reserve of information about Jamaica. Ben enjoyed listening to her soft voice, which seemed to weave itself in and out of the distant rhythm of steel drums drifting over from a beach party at the resort.

After dinner, Carrie cradled a snifter of apricot brandy in both hands without drinking, peering through the dark-amber liquid at the candle flames in the center of the table. Ben leaned over and poured her a cup of aromatic Blue Mountain coffee from an insulated carafe.

"The red snapper was delicious," she said.

"If you hadn't liked it, I planned to rough up the chef," he said straight-faced, and was rewarded with a smile.

Ben looked closely, and fancied that he saw a hint of Price Carmichael in the angle of her nose, and in the gentle arch of her cheekbones. But that was bound to be wishful thinking, because there had been nothing gentle in Price's chiseled features.

He would like to have a photo of Carrie with the glow of candlelight on her face.

"Spare the chef," she said, still smiling.

"We could go into Montego Bay tomorrow," Ben heard himself say. "There's a little place near the straw market—"

"Whoa!" she laughed.

This was only the second time Ben had heard Carrie Washburn laugh. He was wondering what he would have to do to hear it again, when the light in her eyes suddenly seemed to flicker out. She leaned back and raised her chin.

"Ben, this has all been very nice. More than nice." She shot a quick glance past him at the convocation of birds. "It hardly seems real."

"I'm glad you—"

"But don't you think it's time we cut to the chase?" she broke in. "We both know you didn't invite me here for the pleasure of my company."

Carrie had caught him off guard, partly because he was in fact deriving a great deal of pleasure from her company. Ben took a moment to doctor his coffee with cream and sugar, buying time as he made the unwelcome transition between a peculiar sense of contentment, and business.

Then he drew the sheaf of papers from his pocket and placed it on the table, still folded so the cashier's check clipped inside didn't show. With his hands steepled over the neat bundle, he marshaled his most persuasive courtroom tone.

"I'll be honest, Carrie, I hadn't anticipated your almost hostile response when I mentioned Price Carmichael this afternoon."

"There was nothing *almost* about it," though saying that appeared to make her uneasy.

"Do you mind telling me why you feel this way about him?"

Carrie took a deep breath and let it out slowly. She had gone from relaxed and slightly dreamy-eyed in the candlelight, to tense and watchful. Everything about her indicated to Ben that she didn't want to be having this conversation.

"If you have to ask why," she said, sounding sad, "then you must not have known my uncle very well."

Ben shook his head. "I worked for Price since before

Calypso Wind   25

I got out of law school." He fingered the papers. "I'm still working for him as executor of his will."

For a moment, she seemed incapable of unlocking her gaze from his. Ben felt her bewildering tension seize him like a physical force.

"Carrie, what is this problem you seem to have with Price? He was your only living relative, but as far as I know, you never even communicated with him. And every time I mention his name, it's like I'm lighting your fuse."

She flinched. Her cheeks colored, like the blush rising on a peach. She remained perfectly still for a good half-minute, staring at the tablecloth. Then she carefully placed her napkin on the table and gathered herself to leave.

Mentally scrambling, Ben raised both hands to forestall her. He knew very well that Carrie Washburn lived hand-to-mouth. By all rights, the very mention of Price Carmichael's will ought to have her hanging on his every word. Instead, it had had the exact opposite effect.

Her attitude threatened to drive Ben up the wall. For the life of him, he couldn't figure out why that pleased him.

"Look," he said in his most conciliatory tone, "your uncle's will is complicated. If you'll just—"

"If it's so complicated, you should have put more effort into making it simple."

"I didn't prepare it." *I didn't even know about it until three months ago,* Ben added to himself. Just thinking about being kept totally in the dark like that stung. He pressed his hands flat on the table. "If you'll just give me five minutes, I'll explain everything."

He well knew it would take a lot longer than five minutes. But if Carrie would just hang around that long, he was sure he could keep her interested. Not that he had a reason in the world to feel so confident of that when, thus far, nothing else had gone as planned.

Carrie remained perched on the edge of her chair. Taking that as a modestly good sign, Ben said, "Price left a few small cash bequests."

"Let me guess. The chauffeur, the butler, and the upstairs maid." She blushed, apparently embarrassed by her own sharp tone.

"No maid. A cleaning service came in."

She didn't smile, which came as no surprise.

Ben unfolded the sheaf of papers and slipped the cashier's check from its clip. "This is the last of those bequests." *And the most important.* He reached across the table and placed the check face-up in front of her. "That's free and clear, by the way. The inheritance tax has already been taken care of."

Carrie stared at the check, both hands folded in her lap, her tight expression unchanged. After a moment, she blinked several times and the color drained from her face. Then she slowly gripped the edge of the table, fingertips inches from the check, as if she were afraid to touch it.

Calypso Wind

"This . . . this is made out for one hundred thousand dollars," she said in a hushed monotone.

"A drop in the bucket . . . if you want it to be."

She looked dazed. Ben felt a tightness in his chest, seeing how overwhelmed she was by what Price would have considered pocket change. When he placed a hand over hers, she didn't seem to notice.

"The check is yours, Carrie. Call it a down payment. But there's so much more. All you have to do is sign on by the end of the week, and the rest of Price's fortune is yours."

"Sign on?" Her voice sounded like a faint echo.

"Right. Just meet three conditions, and it's all yours."

Her eyes suddenly cleared. She looked suspicious. Sensing his advantage fading fast, Ben charged on.

"One," he said, "you agree to occupy the family mansion in Boston."

Her eyes narrowed.

"Two, you agree to accept the Carmichael estate in its entirety. I have a complete financial statement back at the resort."

Her lips pressed into a white line.

"And three," taking Carrie's attitude toward her uncle into consideration, Ben braced himself for an explosion, "you legally change your last name to Carmichael."

Carrie's jaw dropped, then snapped shut. The explosion didn't happen. Instead, she simply stared at him as a flush rose into her taut cheeks—her blush reminding him of a cuttlefish that displayed its emotions in rapid flashes of color. Then, to Ben's utter dismay, tears welled up in her eyes. She suddenly looked wounded and vulnerable.

That rocked Ben. If the tears actually got loose, he wouldn't know what to do.

This was not in the plan.

"If you don't agree to those conditions by the end of the week," he continued, seeking refuge in the unwritten blueprint that he had prepared for this moment, "the entire Carmichael estate will revert to distant relatives of Price's late wife."

Surely Carrie wouldn't let all that slip through her fingers, Ben thought.

But she didn't bat an eye. She just stared at him with her heartbreakingly beautiful eyes turning to liquid. He wished she would speak. Blow up. Nod. Anything. The brimming tears were about to undo him.

"I've brought the contract that you're required to sign." Ben slid the sheaf of papers across to her and reached for a pen, trying to think positively in the face of her pained silence. "You should read it carefully first."

At long last, she shook her head, the movement jerky like a rusty robot. "I could never take that name. *Ever*." Barely a whisper, but with the power of a thunderbolt.

Ben sat back, the pen slipping from his fingers. Stunned. That's how he felt. He had seen this coming—

Calypso Wind   29

Carrie's total rejection of her uncle's name. But he hadn't believed it would happen, not really, and it still didn't make a lick of sense.

"Why not?" he asked. As recently as that morning, he couldn't have conceived of anyone turning down such wealth. And over a name?

Carrie straightened her shoulders. Blinking back tears, she cleared her throat. "My uncle spoke to me only once in my entire life, Ben. That was five years ago, when I had the audacity to go see him after Mom passed away. Would you like to know what he said to me?"

"Very much." But he had an uneasy feeling that he wouldn't like what she was about to tell him.

She looked down at the table, seeming to struggle for control. "When I told Price Carmichael that his sister . . ." She swallowed, took a slow breath, and started over, her voice steadying. "When I told him, he just looked at me across that aircraft-carrier desk of his and asked what I wanted."

Ben held his breath, distantly aware of waves thudding onto the beach outside, and a busy fluttering of feathers behind him. When Carrie finally spoke again, he had to lean forward to catch the words.

"I was nineteen years old," she whispered. "I was alone. I just wanted—family. But when I told him that, he called me a . . . a gold digger."

Ben rocked back in his chair. Not for one instant did he entertain the possibility that Carrie Washburn was lying—there could be no reason for her to. But she must have misunderstood Price. That had to be it. She had to have taken something the old man said out of context. Price Carmichael was a good man.

"Be reasonable, Carrie. Why would your uncle have structured the will as he did if he didn't genuinely care about you?"

"Maybe he ran out of people who cared about *him*."

"No. He didn't." Not as long as Ben was still alive.

"Then maybe he was just trying to appease his conscience for what he'd done to Mom." Her voice broke on the last word.

That threw Ben. He wanted to ask about her mother, but was afraid that might burst the dam on her tears.

Instead, they stared at each other across the table, the gulf between them even wider than Ben had suspected. The whole idea that they were at opposite poles about the same man left him speechless. He couldn't think of a thing to say that would do anything but drive Carrie's conviction deeper.

"Thank you for a lovely dinner, Ben." Her voice softened with the abrupt change of subject. She glanced past him at the birds, then back at Ben. A crooked smile tilted bravely. "You have a feather in your hair."

He reached up and found a crisp Christmas-green feather with a yellow underside. Impulsively, he held it out to Carrie. Just as impulsively, she took it. With that small exchange, Ben sensed a connection. For some reason, Carrie wasn't lumping him in with how she felt about her uncle. That gave Ben some small hope that he

Calypso Wind   31

still might be able to persuade her to change her mind about the inheritance.

While he was busy mentally formulating his next argument, Carrie slid back her chair and stood.

"It's getting late," she said. "I'm afraid I have an early morning."

He bolted to his feet. "I'll drive you."

She shook her head. "Thanks anyway."

With a strained smile, she turned and stepped through the doorway. Pausing on the wooden deck, she slipped out of her sandals before striking out across the beach.

Feeling a gentle tug at his sleeve, Ben absentmindedly freed himself from a smallish beak as he watched Carrie Washburn walk away into the moonlight.

"Everything okay, mon?" The waiter seemed to materialize out of nowhere.

"Everything's lousy," Ben admitted. "But the food was superb."

He realized the cashier's check was still lying on the table. Ben snatched it up and jammed it into his pocket along with the inheritance contract. By the time he'd signed the credit card receipt, Carrie already had a hefty lead.

Ben set off at a loose jog, then slowed to a brisk walk as he closed the gap between them to a dozen or so yards. The crash of the surf on the long curve of beach and the rhythm of steel drums over at the resort masked the sound of his footsteps. He kept his distance, content to escort Carrie safely home without her knowledge.

He had his work cut out for him. He still couldn't believe she was determined to turn her back on the Carmichael fortune. Carrie had a strong independent streak that he admired, particularly since the private detective he'd hired reported that she was pulling herself through college by her bootstraps.

And that's what worried him. How in blue blazes was he going to bring Carrie Washburn around to accepting her inheritance before the deadline ran out?

The gentle night breeze tugged at her skirt and drew long wisps of her hair toward the sea. She had a graceful walk that seemed to unconsciously match itself to the reggae beat of the drums. Ben didn't have to remind himself that he was alone on a moonlit tropical beach with an attractive woman.

All in all, he observed ruefully, it was about the most unsatisfying walk he had ever experienced.

Chapter Three

The crescent of resort beach, already raked clean of the night's sea wrack, was still mostly deserted in the early dawn. Carrie slipped an oversized tie-dyed T-shirt over her bathing suit as she stood on the postage-stamp sized balcony of her room, watching a lone jogger make his way along the wet sand. He moved in long athletic strides, trailed by one of the island's generic yellow dogs.

There was something familiar about the jogger, but she couldn't quite make him out in the pale light. He was almost even with her—still fifty yards away beyond the resort swimming pool and a narrow stretch of manicured lawn studded with towering pimento trees—before she recognized Ben Ross.

He ran barefooted, stripped to a pair of gray-over-red

jogging shorts, his legs as lean and hard as his upper body. Every now and then, he gestured emphatically as though arguing with himself. He seemed oblivious to the mutt panting along in his wake.

Hugging herself, Carrie watched the unlikely pair until they disappeared beyond a grove of coconut palms down the beach. When she finally turned and went inside, she was surprised to realize she was smiling.

Walking back from the Sand Dollar Restaurant last night, she had been assaulted by a rowdy gang of emotions. Least expected among those was a strong regret that she had probably seen the last of the Boston attorney. Price Carmichael's attorney, she had reminded herself over and over.

Even now, she found it difficult to believe that she actually felt sorry for Ben because she had messed up his grand scheme of things.

Nevertheless, Carrie was proud of herself. Assertiveness wasn't exactly her middle name, so discovering that her principles were made of steel had been a kind of awakening. She could have used the inheritance—considering the pitiful state of her bank account, the "down payment" check alone seemed like vast riches—but it would have come at too high a price.

She could not imagine spending the rest of her life knowing that she had fulfilled Price Carmichael's last wishes. She would *not* adopt his name. Not when in his will, he had tried to buy what she might have given freely, once upon a time. And certainly not after what he had done to her mother.

With a sigh, she grabbed her straw tote bag off the closet shelf and headed down to the breakfast buffet.

Hunched over the glass-topped patio table, Mark Hanes scowled at his breakfast plate. "Carrie, what *is* this stuff?" he muttered.

"Spinach."

"For *breakfast?*" He jabbed his fork at the mound of coarse greens. "Looks like it came out of a lawnmower bag."

"Mark, you did order the authentic Jamaican breakfast," Carrie reminded him, trying to sound perky. But she was embarrassed by Mark's open disdain for the delightful island cuisine. She was also worried sick over the ominous news that Lana had dropped on her not twenty minutes ago. "Be adventurous. The spinach is delicious, and you haven't even tasted the crab cakes."

Mark poked around at his breakfast some more, then shoved his plate aside, scowling. The accountant had been grumpy ever since he came down for breakfast, and yet he had insisted on sharing a table with Carrie. She wondered if he had been at the Sand Dollar last night and had seen her dining with Ben Ross. Stealing a glance at Mark across the small table, it occurred to her that she might be looking at the face of jealousy.

Carrie fought back a frown of her own, replacing it with a practiced tourguide smile. She had never dealt with a jealous client before, and didn't quite know where to begin. *As if you don't have a lot worse things to worry about—such as losing your job.*

A burst of laughter drew her attention across the patio to where Sybil and Arnold Rodgers sat at a poolside table. Clad in matching green-and-white dashikis and sturdy walking shorts, they had already downed a hearty Jamaican breakfast, complete with fruit plate. Now they were pouring over a copy of the *Jamaica Daily News*.

Now there is a couple who knows how to get the biggest bang for their vacation buck, Carrie thought.

From the looks of their sensible walking shoes, she guessed that they planned to join the morning's excursion to the Montego Bay straw market. Arnold and Sybil were bargain-shopping fiends, ever on the lookout for gifts for their many grandkids.

"Uhm . . . say," Mark leaned closer and lowered his voice. "I've heard a rumor."

Carrie tensed. She hadn't told a soul—not even Lana yet—about the inheritance she had turned down. Only Ben Ross knew about it, and if he'd had the audacity to blab it around the resort. . . .

Mark cupped a hand over his mouth and murmured, "I understand there was a burglary here at Calypso Beach last night."

She stared at him as it slowly soaked in that she had charged off in the wrong direction. She mentally retraced her steps, dragging a burden of guilt over having been so quick to cast Ben Ross in a bad light.

Carrie cleared her throat, twice. "That's true, Mark. But if you keep your valuables in the resort safe when you're away from your room, as you should at any hotel, you have nothing to worry about."

"Oh, I'm not worried." His lip curled as he shifted his gaze to take in the scattered diners on the patio. "I'm just wondering 'who done it.'"

The Rodgers duo had left their table and headed toward the broad doorway leading into the lobby. Carrie watched them for a moment, counting the number of times they had come to Jamaica with Galaxy Tours during the two years that she had been working for Lana. They invariably scooped up so many "bargains" that they had to ship a crate or two of purchases back home, paying heavy duty charges.

For just a second, Carrie wondered what the duty was on stolen property. Then her face heated. She liked Sybil and Arnold a lot. She couldn't believe she could even begin to suspect them of being anything other than a sweet, fun-loving retired couple.

"Me tart pretty ooman be gawn!"

Carrie couldn't help laughing at the familiar flurry of musical island patois, even before she turned and looked up at Winston Brown. The tall, lanky waiter grinned down at her, twirling the keys to his mobile snack bar, his longish hair cornrowed in an artistic zigzag pattern studded with plastic beads.

"Winston, you're the only person I know who speaks patois with a New Jersey accent."

"Shh!" he cautioned, still grinning. "If the tourists find out, the tips fall off." He dropped the patois, but his lilting island accent remained.

She reached across to Mark. "Winston's from Newark," she explained. "He comes down here to work at the resorts every year during the season."

"Really?" Mark said. "Sounds like a killer commute."

Winston shrugged. "Two kids getting ready for college. You know how it is."

"Afraid not," Mark said. "No kids."

"Ah." Winston sighed heavily as though he had just received tragic news, then took a step away from the table. "Well, it's back to the grindstone."

Carrie watched him amble off across the flagstone patio toward the red-and-gold canopied cart that he spent all day wheeling back and forth along the sidewalk parallel to the beach.

"You're serious?" Mark said. "The guy leaves his family in the States and comes all the way down here to work?"

She nodded. "That isn't as unusual as you'd think. The tips during tourist season make it worthwhile. Besides, Winston was born here. His kids were born in New Jersey, so he's sort of rooted in both cultures."

Carrie sighed. "I razz Winston a lot about having to work in a tropical paradise, but he misses his family terribly. Once he gets his kids through college, he and some of his friends want to save up and start their own business back in the States."

Carrie didn't mention that she was pretty much in the same boat as Winston, only she was working her way through college.

She felt a drumming sensation on the back of her wrought-iron chair, and tilted her head back to see who was standing behind her. She almost choked when she found Ben Ross towering over her, clad in electric-blue swimtrunks with a Calypso Beach towel slung over one broad shoulder.

"Morning," he said cheerfully. "I trust you slept soundly last night."

A light seemed to glint in his hazel eyes. Carrie had a nagging feeling that he was mocking her, certain that the inheritance that she had turned down had kept her wide awake. She wasn't about to give him the satisfaction of knowing that it had.

"Slept like a baby," she said, crossing her fingers under the table.

He gave her a long, steady look, the corners of his lips slightly curled. After a moment, she grew nervous under his scrutiny. At the same time, she enjoyed every second of it. A warm, liquid sensation flowed through her body, leaving her skin tingling.

"What can I do for you, Ben?" she asked, then

reminded herself that he was not a member of the Galaxy tour.

Tiny crow's feet deepened at the corners of his eyes as the gentle sea breeze riffled his hair. He seemed to consider her question for a long time before apparently choosing not to answer it.

"I hope you didn't find dinner last night too... upsetting," he said.

"Not at all," she said, bending the truth while hammering away at her smile. "I thoroughly enjoyed myself."

Ben rubbed the knuckle of one thumb across his chin, the copper chips in his eyes shining. "Are you sure?"

"Positive."

"Then you wouldn't mind repeating it."

"What?"

"Dinner, of course. Do you happen to know Sam Rivers?"

"*The* Sam Rivers? The actor?"

He nodded.

"You can't be serious." As if Ben Ross could actually believe for one instant that she rubbed elbows with famous movie stars.

"Well," he said, "Sam's the friend I was telling you about—the one with the place over near Half Moon Bay. The dinner would be at his place."

Things began to go a little out of focus for Carrie.

Was Ben really inviting her to break bread with the hottest box office heartthrob in the entire Western world? And not just any old heartthrob. Carrie had been a devoted fan of Sam Rivers's since high school.

"When?" Her voice sounded small and far away.

"Later this week. I haven't asked Sam and Trish when they want to invite us."

"Trish?"

"Sam's wife."

Sam and Trish. Ben knew them by their first names. And he was inviting himself and Carrie to their house before even asking them. Impossible.

"Then you'll go?" he asked.

Carrie had struggled for years just to keep her head above water. Now she was just a nod away from mingling with Golden People. *Sam and Trish.* She couldn't help it. She nodded.

"Great!" Ben smiled, and brushed her shoulder with one fingertip. "Meanwhile, how about a swim?"

She didn't need water—she was already in over her head, floundering. Carrie realized that she'd just allowed herself to get sucked into spending another evening with Price Carmichael's attorney. And to her utter amazement, she was looking forward to it.

"I can't," she managed. But, oh, how she wanted to dive into the crystal-blue sea with Ben. She was even dressed for it beneath her baggy T-shirt.

"Ten minutes," he insisted.

"Can't." This time the word carried slightly more conviction as she glanced at her watch. "I'm due to take a group of Galaxy clients horseback riding."

Ben didn't miss a beat. "How about tomorrow morning?"

"Sorry. Tomorrow, I take the group that doesn't go this morning."

He sighed without losing his smile. "Okay, I get the message. I'm on my own for the day."

Carrie reached up and gave his hand a consoling pat, then jerked her hand back down to her lap. Something about Ben Ross made her continually want to run away from him and toward him at the same time.

He gave her his Huckleberry Finn grin, and for a couple of seconds Carrie forgot that he had any connection whatsoever with Price Carmichael. Then that reality came storming back, along with the certainty that Ben still had hopes of getting her to sign that blasted inheritance contract.

Her heart sank. She wished Ben could have been interested in her just for her own sake. While she was at it—might as well dream big—she fervently wished that he had no connection with her late uncle.

She pointed off down the beach. "See the young man in the orange trunks standing in the surf?"

Ben shaded his eyes. "The one with the dreadlocks?"

"His name is Gordon Darnell, and that's his glass-bottom boat anchored in the water."

"It could use a paint job."

Calypso Wind

"If you're a good swimmer," she said, "Gordon will take you out for a look at the reef."

"Why would I need to swim at all with a glass-bottomed boat?"

"It's been known to sink. You'll need to hurry before resort security makes him tow it farther off down the beach."

Noting Ben's expression, Carrie hurried to add, "Or he'll rent you a board and show you how to windsurf."

A couple of other beach entrepreneurs were already out on the water demonstrating their brightly-sailed boards, cutting graceful courses across the waves. They made it look deceptively easy.

Carrie blinked away an image of Ben Ross skimming swiftly across the dazzling water, his muscular limbs flexing easily with the strain.

"Calypso Beach has its own rental equipment," he said. "Why would I want to take a risk on Darnell's junk?"

"He needs your business, Ben. Just tell him I sent you. He'll fix you up."

Ben gave her a long, appraising look, then shifted his gaze back down the beach toward Gordon Darnell. He seemed to be turning something over in his mind. After a moment, he nodded almost imperceptibly.

"Okay, I'll give it a shot." He patted her lightly on the shoulder. "Don't go getting saddle sores."

Carrie watched him stride purposefully across the patio toward the beach.

Behind her, a chair scraped the flagstones. She glanced around at Mark Hanes, who had risen. She had forgotten all about him.

"I'm sorry, Mark!" She hopped up, fumbling for her tote bag. "I should have introduced you. That was Ben Ross, a Boston—"

"That's all right," Mark interrupted, squinting after the departing attorney.

When he finally shifted his gaze to her, Carrie realized that he was furious.

The next morning, Ben sucked it up and gave four more strong breaststrokes before letting a shallow wave carry him the rest of the way in to the beach. Preoccupied, he had stupidly ventured out much farther from shore than he had intended. His muscles burned as he waded in through the foaming surf. But it felt good to have worked off some of the tension that had built up over the past twenty-four hours.

Three yellow dogs waited on the damp sand at the edge of the surf. Raking wet hair off his forehead, Ben picked up a chunk of driftwood and flung it down the beach for them. Their heads turned in unison to follow its course, but none of them budged. Then all three heads turned back, and they wagged at him.

"Lassie, go home," he murmured as he peered into the angled morning sun toward the resort's beachside patio.

The patio had been empty when he entered the water

shortly after dawn. It was crowded now, but he quickly spotted Carrie seated at the same table as on the previous morning. She was having breakfast with the same guy, Ben noted with a pensive frown. He was sorely tempted to join them, but decided against it. He needed time alone with Carrie. Time to find out what made her tick.

Admit it, Ross—you just want to be with her.

Ben shook his head. He had chased Carrie Washburn down to Jamaica with nothing more in mind than getting her quick signature on a piece of paper. It made no sense at all that he should suddenly have become so enthralled by the warmth of her chestnut eyes, and the way her lower lip twitched when she was upset.

Abruptly, he turned away from the patio and slogged down the beach, trailed by the three dogs.

"Hey, mon! Ready for a ride in my very fine glass-bottom boat?"

Ben halted. Preoccupied again, he had almost walked head-on into Gordon Darnell. The reed-thin hustler beckoned toward his dilapidated boat riding gently in the surf a dozen yards away.

"I'll pass," Ben said, continuing along the beach.

"Then how 'bout a sail board to catch the nice wind? You did so very fine on it yesterday."

Ben kept shaking his head, smiling. Darnell was too good-natured to be annoying. Ben had to admit that he was as impressed as Carrie seemed to be by the youth's drive, not to mention his intelligence.

Unwilling to stray far from his boat and windsurf board Darnell raised his voice one last time as Ben walked away. "Whatever you need, mon, you just ask me. Even 'bout your Ca-ro-line." Darnell sang out the name.

Ben walked on for several paces before the name registered, stopping him in his tracks. He turned and walked back toward Darnell past the three trailing mutts, who also reversed course.

"Caroline?"

Darnell gave a deep nod. "Miss Caroline Washburn. You see, I know everything 'bout this place." He made a sweeping gesture that took in much more than just the Calypso Beach Resort.

"Interesting." Ben folded his arms. "How about if we start with Carrie?"

"Okay." Darnell eyed him speculatively.

"If the information comes with a price tag, you'll have to trust me." Ben indicated his wet swimtrunks. "As you can see, I'm not carrying a wallet."

"No problem. Carrie said to fix you up, mon." The youth matched Ben's stance, folding his arms over his bony chest. "That makes your credit top-rate."

Ben was doubly intrigued. First, that Carrie was held in such high esteem by a local beach hustler. And second, that Darnell offered a convenient credit plan.

"What can you tell me about Carrie Washburn that I don't already know?" Ben asked.

The young man sighed. "It's so sad. She maybe

won't come back with the Galaxy Tours lady after this time," he said with what appeared to be genuine regret.

"Why not?"

"Because of the teef."

Teef? Ben scratched his chin. He had always struggled with the island dialect. "Oh . . . thief. What thief?"

"The one that took tings from the rooms the last time Galaxy came to Calypso Beach. He's doing it again dis time. So resort police don't want Galaxy to ever come back."

Ben slowly lowered his arms. "Are you telling me the tour company Carrie works for is being run out of the resort?"

"Maybe not just yet." Darnell squinted his eyes in a shrewd expression. "Maybe dey don't have enough proof yet. Maybe Calypso Beach is a little afraid Carrie's boss will sue dem if dey be wrong, mon."

"God in heaven."

A cold, hollow sensation settled into Ben's belly. That's all he needed—for Carrie Washburn to get caught up in a scandal. Price had been very specific about that in his will. A scandal would put the inheritance forever beyond Carrie's reach.

He looked back toward the patio, awash in brilliant morning sunlight. His gaze fixed on the empty chair where Carrie had been seated only minutes ago. For a painful moment a door that Ben had bolted shut long ago swung open, and his thoughts drifted back to his own past. Back before Price Carmichael stepped into his life and changed it forever.

Ben gave his head another shake, then wiped both hands down his face as if to scrape away the memory. A residue of unease remained.

Forget the past. It's over.

As if anything in a man's life was ever truly over.

He refocused on the real problem at hand, namely Carrie Washburn. He was determined to get her back to Boston . . . back to her roots. But just getting her there wasn't going to be good enough. Not by a long shot.

Carrie's good name had to be protected at all costs. Beacon Hill society loved nothing better than a juicy scandal. If word ever got out connecting Price Carmichael's heir to resort thefts, however indirectly, society mavens would never let Carrie live it down.

Chapter Four

A big charter bus carrying a fresh load of resort guests slowed on the highway, air brakes wheezing, and turned in through the front gate. Carrie herded her Galaxy group to the side of the broad driveway as the bus lumbered over a series of speed bumps, dubbed "silent policemen" by the locals.

Mark Hanes trudged along at her side, his nose painted white with sunblock, scowling in the dazzling sunlight.

"We could catch a shuttle," he suggested. "Be there in half the time."

"The stable is just a short walk up the road, Mark. The hike will loosen us up for the ride." Carrie walked backward for a few paces as she did a quick head count. "Think of it as part of the total experience."

She wished Mark would lighten up. He had stuck with her like a second shadow all morning, as if he couldn't enjoy one moment on this beautiful island without her guidance.

Carrie led the way through the front gate, where Lester Darnell squatted next to a basket of succulent, freshly-cut aloe vera leaves. A born salesman, Gordon Darnell's little brother broke into a wide grin when he saw her. But after a sharp-eyed inspection of her group, he didn't bother getting up. Lester knew his market, which consisted mainly of incoming sun-burn victims.

They both knew he would do a brisk trade in the sunburn-soothing leaves when the group returned later in the day. No matter how much Carrie harped on the use of sunblock, there were always a handful of clients who insisted on going home fried, as if a first-degree burn were an official authentication of their vacation.

"Shouldn't that kid be in school?" Mark asked as they headed up the road.

She smiled. "Lester has dreams. He hustles an education just as hard as he hustles a buck. With a lucky break, he'll end up with his share of both."

Carrie hoped that wasn't wishful thinking on her part. She admired the Darnell brothers' dedication to the free-enterprise system. But with five siblings and a widowed mother to look after, it was difficult to see how they could ever manage to get a real toehold on the economic ladder.

Mark's hand brushed hers. Carrie instinctively

slipped her hand into her jeans' pocket out of reach, suspecting the contact hadn't been as accidental as he would have it seem. She thought she might like Mark a lot better if he would give her a little breathing space.

"Carrie, dear."

She glanced back at Rita Sausson, a middle-aged secretary with thick glasses. Rita's nose was already turning red from the tropical sun.

"I know what the schedule says." Rita rolled her eyes as if the tour's printed schedule were a horribly incorrigible brat. "But some of us would like to go in to Montego Bay before Wednesday."

"Then by all means, go ahead." Carrie smiled encouragement.

Rita backed off instantly. Like so many tour group members, she found leaving the herd daunting.

They crossed the two-lane highway and moved down a narrow dirt track. At the foot of the track stood a low, flat-roofed wooden hut that served as the riding-stable office. The nearby corral was empty. A dozen horses were already saddled and waiting, tied to trees and posts scattered around the dusty stable yard.

Carrie's entire group stopped and gaped at the animals in stunned silence.

Mark was the first to speak. "Ponies."

"No, they're real horses," Carrie assured him. "They're just wiry little guys."

"They look like they haven't been fed in a month. You can count their ribs."

"It's the tropical climate, Mark. If they carried an ounce of excess fat, it would probably kill them. Relax everyone. Trust me, they're healthy as . . . well, healthy as horses." She smiled at the group's collective disbelief. "Go ahead and take your pick. I'll go find William."

Fists on his hips, Mark shook his head in disgust. But then he sidled over to a bay mare that listed to one side in the shade of a tree, her neck draped over a neighbor's withers. Unless Carrie was badly mistaken, both horses were snoring.

Welcome to the tropics, she thought, grinning in anticipation of her clients' coming surprise.

She was halfway to the hut when William stepped out. As lean and leathery as his tough little Jamaican horses, the stable owner tipped his cowboy hat at her and crammed a wad of bills into a pocket of his jeans.

"Up the mountain and down again, Miss Washburn?" He sounded for all the world like a proper English gentleman.

"That ought to just about take care of everyone, William."

Sauntering into the sun-baked yard, Winston began helping women into saddles and adjusting stirrups. He moved unhurriedly from mount to mount, stroking each animal as he went. As Carrie turned toward a horse that was snoozing with its head propped in the fork of a tree, another figure emerged from the shadowed interior of the hut.

Ben Ross leaned casually against the weathered doorjamb and smiled at her, looking fit and athletic in faded cutoffs and an untucked polo shirt. He didn't stop smiling as he raised a can of cola to his lips and took a long swig.

"What are you doing here?" she asked.

"Isn't it obvious?"

Carrie watched as he flipped the empty can into a rusty barrel outside the door and strode over to one of the few remaining unchosen mounts. He rattled the bridle to awaken the sleeping steed, then swung nimbly into the saddle without bothering with the stirrups.

As luck would have it, his horse stood near the one Mark had selected. From Carrie's vantage point, the comparison that such close proximity invited was hardly to Mark's advantage.

Ben slouched comfortably in the saddle, hands resting loosely on his muscular thighs, totally at ease. Mark sat ironing-board straight, gripping the saddle horn, looking so out of his element that Carrie wondered again why he had ever signed up for the ride. She couldn't help feeling embarrassed for the accountant.

Once everyone was mounted, William swung onto his usual black gelding. Carrie watched with interest as he scanned the group for a likely point-rider. As was his habit, William would bring up the rear, brooking no stragglers.

Finally, he motioned to Ben. "Would you kindly set the pace?"

Ben obligingly turned his horse toward the well-beaten path up the mountain. With a snort, the animal went from a state of total inertia to a spirited trot in all of two paces. Ben appeared startled for just an instant, but didn't try to hold his horse back.

Carrie's horse fell in behind him with little encouragement from her. The ten other horses joined the charge with a clattering of hooves on rocks, eliciting startled cries from their riders.

Ben rode with his long legs wrapped around his mount's rangy body, the stirrups flopping free. As the rocky trail steepened, Carrie began to wonder when he would slow the pace. A short while later, she realized Ben was content to let his horse set the pace—a relentless, teeth-jarring trot—while he enjoyed the scenery.

Riding close behind, captivated by his careless grace, Carrie was oblivious to the vibrant tropical heat until she saw him fan his shirttail in the breeze. The trail switched back and forth up the face of the mountain, presenting evermore expansive views of the lush lowlands they were leaving behind, but she couldn't seem to keep her gaze off this new aspect of Ben Ross.

At a steep bend in the trail, her horse stumbled slightly on a loose rock. That was just enough to distract Carrie's attention. She suddenly remembered they weren't alone. Twisting around in the saddle, she glanced back at the rest of the riding party.

Immediately behind her, Mark bounced along in his saddle, still maintaining a death-grip on the saddle horn, his flushed face twisted in an anxious expression. Saddle sores in the making, she thought.

Out of consideration for the energetic pace being set up front, William apparently had decided to cut some slack. The rest of the group was strung out down the mountain, negotiating the steady climb as best they could. Everyone except Mark seemed to be enjoying themselves immensely.

Carrie returned her attention to the path ahead just in time to see Ben whip his shirt off over his head. The muscles in his back rippled in the brilliant sunlight. Once again, she felt herself lose track of time and space.

The trail widened abruptly, then leveled out onto a grassy knoll. One by one, the horses slowed to a walk as they approached a water trough in front of a squat tin-roofed shack. Ben dismounted at the trough. Carrie slid off her saddle next to him and stood flexing her knees, breathing hard, trying to get her land legs back. As usual, she observed, the horses hadn't even broken a sweat.

"I assume this was our destination," he said, glancing around.

Catching herself staring at tiny beads of sweat glistening on Ben's broad chest, Carrie looked away as Mark rode up and clumsily dismounted. The accountant frowned, his gaze dancing suspiciously between her and Ben.

Carrie quickly moved away from both men.

"Cold drinks for sale over here," she announced, pointing to the shack as the rest of the riders straggled in.

A shutter swung open under the porch overhang, and an old man leaned out of the opening. Hot and thirsty, Carrie plucked a dripping can of soda from a plastic ice chest on the porch, paid the proprietor, and wandered over to sit in the shade of a wind-tattered banana tree. The breeze at the top of the mountain was heavenly.

"Mind if I join you?"

Carrie glanced up as Ben's shadow passed over her. He sank down beside her, crossed his long legs Indian style, and busied himself with the pull-tab on his own can of pop.

She eyed him furtively. His face and upper body were flushed from the heat. Up close, she could smell sunscreen melting into the musky scent of his aftershave lotion. Sitting so close to him suddenly made her nervous, but she realized that she didn't necessarily want him to move away.

And that made her even more nervous.

"What a place." Ben spoke in a near-whisper.

Carrie followed his gaze down the verdant mountainside all the way to a broad expanse of pale beach. Beyond an undulating white ribbon of surf, the turquoise sea stretched to the far horizon. The breeze sighing through the banana leaves mimicked the sound of the distant surf, so it was easy to imagine that they were hearing the waves rolling onto the hot sand.

The first time she had taken in that panoramic vista a

few years ago, Carrie had also felt an unaccountable impulse to whisper. Now she had a strange sense that she was seeing it for the first time. The view had never seemed more breathtaking than it did at that moment.

Over at the shack, Mark stood with a foot propped up on a wooden bench, inspecting what was probably a saddle sore on the inside of his thigh. After a moment, he turned his head in such a way that Carrie was certain he was watching her and Ben from the corner of his eye. She sighed. She didn't want to be rude, but she found herself hoping Mark wouldn't decide to join them.

Ben slipped a blade of grass through the space between his front teeth as he seemed to take in every little detail of the mountaintop. So it came as no surprise to Carrie when he pointed his soda can off to their right, where the upper part of a weathered stone structure was just visible beyond the crest of the hill.

"What's that?" he asked.

"An old church. It was built with stone ballast from slave ships."

He frowned deeply, and stared at it for a long while.

Carrie watched him, wondering if he might be doing what she always did when she saw that church. It was hard not to reach way down into her collective conscience to make a connection with those terrible words—slave ships.

"Ow!" Carrie bolted to her feet, hopping around and swatting at the inside of her left knee. "Something's biting me!"

Ben grabbed her, sat her down hard, and clamped a hand to her knee, grinding the denim harshly.

"Ow!" she howled. "It's on fire!"

Kneeling beside her, he dug out a miniature Swiss Army knife that looked absurdly small in his big hands. Unfolding a tiny blade, he quickly sliced through the denim of her jeans as if it were butter.

As a small crowd gathered, Ben reached through the opening and gingerly pulled out a squashed bug that looked as if it had once been able to fly.

Ambling over from the refreshment shack, William leaned in to take a look. With a soft whistle, he said, "A wass."

Ben glanced up at him. "Is it dangerous?"

William shook his head. "Just painful."

"Tell me about it," Carrie said through clenched teeth.

Ben put away the knife and examined the site of the sting. An inflamed blister the size of a pencil eraser was already forming. His tender touch helped to distract Carrie from the sensation that a flaming match was being held to her knee.

"Well," he said, "we'd better get you back to the resort infirmary."

He took her arm and started to help her to her feet. Mark stepped out of the crowd and claimed her other arm. It immediately became apparent to Carrie that the two men weren't helping her in exactly the same direction. Suddenly, she felt like a chunk of meat caught in a tug-of-war between two hungry wolves.

"My leg isn't broken, guys." She managed to wrench herself free. "I can manage on my own, thank you."

Mark looked abashed. Ben seemed more amused.

With as much dignity as she could muster while trying not to wail, Carrie strolled off toward her horse.

Near the end of the corridor just off the lobby, Ben held open the smoked-glass door to the infirmary. Still holding her chin high, Carrie limped inside. Pain-lines etched her face, but she hadn't let out a peep all the way down the mountain.

Dearly wishing he could lend her a hand, Ben reluctantly refrained from so much as laying a finger on her. His self-restraint was born of trial-and-error. When he had tried to help Carrie off her horse back at the stable, she had nearly bitten his head off. Not that he blamed her. She was hurting, and trying her best not to show it.

Besides, her explosion had scared off the Galaxy client—Mark somebody—who had been hanging around her like a lost puppy.

The stark-white infirmary was already occupied by an older couple in wet bathing suits, and a nurse in a crisp blue uniform. The man was seated on the examination table, one bare foot cradled in his companion's arms.

"Carrie!" the woman cried as Carrie and Ben entered.

"Sybil." Carrie nodded to her and eased into a chair in the corner. "What happened to you, Arnold?"

"Tangled with a danged spiny urchin while snorkeling." Arnold indicated his big toe. "Hurt like blue blazes. What about you?"

"Stung by a wass."

"A wasp?" Sybil echoed.

"W-a-s-s." Carrie spelled it out for her. "Feels like a wasp with a bad attitude."

Arnold retrieved his foot from his wife's grasp and slid down off the table onto the wet, sand-streaked tile floor. "Well, the nurse is all yours. She fixed me right up."

Sybil fluttered a hand over her chest. "This certainly has been an exciting trip. First the burglary, and now this."

Ben watched Carrie's sun-flushed face go pale. He didn't feel so great himself. Clearly, word of the burglary that Gordon Darnell had told him about had become common knowledge. That didn't bode well for keeping a lid on the scandal.

"I suppose it happens in all the best places, doesn't it, dear?" Sybil helped her husband to the door. "Arnie and I are just glad it wasn't our room that was broken into."

Arnold tugged his sagging bathing trunks up over his protruding belly and opened the door for his wife. "We're too smart for crooks. Don't leave easy-pickings lying around in our room."

He slapped the nylon fanny pack strapped around

Sybil's stout waist, and then the pair disappeared into the corridor.

"They seemed to be in a hurry to leave," Ben said, watching them leave.

"Don't take it personally," Carrie said. "Sybil and Arnold don't let grass grow under their feet when they vacation."

Still, Ben noticed that Carrie frowned pensively at the closing door. Then she shrugged as though dismissing a troubling thought, and hobbled over to take her turn on the examination table.

Fifteen minutes later, Ben escorted Carrie into the elevator. The pain-lines on her face had softened, leaving her with a slightly dazed expression. Whatever the nurse had injected her with must have provided immediate relief. It had also left her a little wobbly in the knees, and she unabashedly clung to Ben's arm for support.

"Are you all right?" he asked.

No response.

She rocked back and forth, smiling peacefully as the elevator rose. By the time the elevator doors glided open on her floor, Ben had noticed that Carrie was half asleep on her feet. At least she was no longer in pain, he thought, grateful for that much.

Ben steered her out of the elevator. "Do you have your key card?"

Carrie plucked it out of her shirt pocket.

"What's your room number?" he asked.

She had to mumble it twice before he caught it. He didn't dare let go of her. She kept trying to veer off to the right, as if her legs were out of alignment. This struck her as outrageously funny. Ben found it less so. He managed to keep her walking despite her convulsive laughter, but it wasn't easy.

At the door to her room, he took her shoulders and turned her to face him. The Rodgers had been preying on his mind ever since they left the infirmary. He didn't care what Carrie had said about grass not growing under the couple's feet—Ben hadn't liked the way they'd skedaddled as soon as he and Carrie arrived.

Maybe he was becoming paranoid where Carrie Washburn was concerned. But whenever he was with her, he felt compelled to keep watch over his shoulder. Even an elderly couple had come under his suspicion. He had to get this situation buttoned down before it got completely out of hand.

"Look, Carrie, you need to get off this island." He gave her a gentle shake, trying to get her to focus on him. "Today."

Her eyes cleared a little. She looked puzzled. "Why?"

"The burglaries. If the resort management is on target about the thief being a client of Galaxy Tours, your reputation could be smeared by association." At least, that would be the collective judgment on Beacon Hill, where

Calypso Wind   63

old-line high society wasn't known for cutting any slack. "Let me arrange for a flight out this afternoon."

She frowned at his chest for a moment, then tilted her head way back and squinted up at him. "No. Absolutely not. I couldn't run off and leave Lana in a lurch. No way, no how." Then she yawned into the back of her hand.

"Okay, okay," he grumbled, brushing a honey-colored tress off her cheek. "Get some sleep. We'll talk about it later."

Where Carrie's mile-wide loyalty streak was concerned, Ben already knew he was spinning his wheels. He admired her steadfast devotion to her employer—to anyone she befriended, most likely—but for just one day, he wished she could be fickle.

He opened the door and ushered her inside. Compared with his suite one floor below, her room was cramped, but she kept everything in its place. No clothes thrown around on the bed or dresser. No shoes scattered on the floor.

Loyal and shipshape—that's my Carrie.

Ben halted. *My Carrie?*

He smiled at himself, bemused by how quickly Carrie Washburn had come to seem like a part of his life. Then again, she was Price Carmichael's niece. Perhaps it was only natural that Ben should feel so protective of his mentor's sole living relative.

"Come on," he said, marching Carrie to the bed and

sitting her down. "Get some shut-eye. You'll feel better by this evening."

"I feel just dandy, Ben."

She toppled backwards. As soon as her head hit the spread, she gave a sigh and was out like a light.

Ben gently lifted her feet onto the bed, eased off her sneakers, and covered her legs with a corner of the spread. She sighed again, sinking ever deeper into sleep. He watched her for several minutes, marveling. With her features totally relaxed, she had an almost childlike beauty.

Innocence, he thought. She has a look of pure, untainted innocence.

And yet, beneath that innate innocence lurked a deep wellspring of strength and stamina. Carrie was putting herself through college, one hard-scrabble semester at a time. She had her eye on the mountaintop, and the will to climb as long as she had to in order to reach the top. And she was doing it alone.

Without thinking, Ben reached out to stroke her cheek, but drew his hand back at the last second. Touching her while she slept would be an invasion of her privacy. When she sighed once again, so did he. Then he smiled, though he figured he had plenty to worry about—the looming scandal and Price Carmichael's fortune, just to name a couple.

At last, Ben gave a soft whistle through his teeth and shook his head. More than anything, he wanted to bend over and brush Carrie's smooth forehead with his lips, and trace the curve of her cheek with the back of a finger. But he had learned a long time ago that he didn't always get what he wanted in life.

"Sleep tight," he murmured.

Without taking his gaze off her, he backed across the room and out the door. Before leaving, he made sure the door was locked.

Chapter Five

The sun angled low toward the horizon. With his elbows planted on a small table on the lattice-covered patio outside the Calypso Beach lounge, Ben was barely aware of the approach of a spectacular tropical sunset.

A frosty glass of iced tea sat untouched in front of him, leaving a wet ring on the glass-topped table. Every now and then, he unclasped his hands, refolded them in reverse, and rested his chin back on his knuckles. In the six hours and forty-odd minutes since he left Carrie's room, Price Carmichael's niece hadn't been out of his thoughts for so much as a millisecond.

Ben hissed through his teeth and took a long swig of tea that didn't help quell the turmoil in his mind one bit. He had come to Jamaica to do a job. But somewhere between the time that Carrie had been stung by the wass, and the moment he had tucked her into her bed, something inside him had shifted. He suddenly wanted to take Carrie in his arms and protect her from the world, as if she would stand for that for one instant.

And yet, that's just what he had to do—protect Carrie from losing what was rightfully hers. In his will, Price Carmichael had entrusted Ben with that responsibility. Until now, Ben had not realized the crushing weight of that duty.

"I don't know what you're chewing on, fella. But it sure looks serious."

Ben straightened as a tall, slender woman slid into the chair across from him. She had on a low-cut purple evening dress that clung to her like the peel on a Tokay grape. She had terrific legs, which she went to great pains to display beneath the glass-topped table. Ben found that he had no interest at all in the show.

"You're Ben Ross, aren't you?" she said.

He nodded.

"I'm Lana Fuller, Ben. Carrie's boss." She toyed with a long necklace made of black coral beads shaped like tiny fishes. "I hear you rescued a damsel in distress today."

"Carrie was stung by an antisocial bug. She was definitely in distress, but I didn't exactly rescue her."

Lana chuckled. "That isn't the way my clients tell it. I got the impression from Sybil Rodgers that you barged into the infirmary with Carrie in your heroic arms."

Ben looked at her askance. "Carrie walked in on her own."

"Ah." Lana glanced around, lips twitching in a barely muted smirk. "Carrie isn't in her room. I thought she might be down here with you."

"She is in her room," he said evenly. "The nurse gave her an injection to kill the pain. She's probably still sound asleep."

Lana watched him for a moment, then relaxed and stopped trying to interest him with her leg show. Ben had to admit that she was an attractive woman, from her impeccable makeup to her frosted-pink pedicure. She had a fashion-model figure, with the straight back and almost stately bearing of a prima ballerina. But when he compared her with simple, unadorned Carrie Washburn, Lana didn't hold a candle.

She waggled her beads at him. "I have a date this evening, Ben. Otherwise, I might have wasted a lot of effort on you."

"Wasted?"

"I can spot the signs. Methinks you're already infatuated with little Carrie."

That took him aback, partly because he had been thinking pretty much the same thing. He was troubled by the realization that his emotions might be that transparent.

"*Little* Carrie?" he said.

Lana shrugged. "I don't know why, but I've always thought of her that way."

Calypso Wind 69

It dawned on Ben that, in the beginning, he had, too. He attributed that error in judgment to Carrie's deceptively delicate features. He found himself making further comparisons between the two women.

Lana Fuller was as flashy as the blaze of coral sunset spreading across the horizon behind her. In contrast, Carrie was a silvery slice of moon, the hidden parts of her even more tantalizing than what was visible.

Ben shifted sideways on his chair, astonished by the uncharacteristic flight of fancy. Wondering what on earth was coming over him, he dispelled the fantasy by grabbing at the first nuts-and-bolts topic that came to mind.

"I hear the resort is having problems with burglaries," he said, tactfully leaving unspoken the rumored connection to Galaxy Tours' clients.

Lana nodded vaguely and gazed off across the patio as if the burglaries were of little consequence to her. Ben detected a slight tightening of the tiny muscles at the corners of her eyes and mouth, and knew better.

His courtroom curiosity surfaced.

He was trying to decide if Lana would tolerate some discreet interrogation when she suddenly let go of her beads and waved at someone.

Ben turned to watch Mark what's-his-face wind his way toward them through the scattered tables. As Mark drew near, Ben rose to offer his hand. He couldn't help noticing that the man's ash-blond hair seemed to have taken on a peculiar orange cast, the way dye jobs sometimes did under the tropical sun. He found it difficult not to stare.

"I've been trying to ring Carrie's room," Mark said with obvious concern. "I'm concerned about her."

"So was I, but she's fine." Lana explained the side effects of the painkiller Carrie had received. "According to Ben, our girl is in bed, far away in dreamland."

Mark turned a narrow, appraising eye on Ben.

Ben eyed him back, rising to the silent challenge. He felt a slow smile coming on as he realized he was engaging in territorial male posturing with Mark. Ben stretched himself to his full height, feeling all of seventeen years old and having a ripping good time of it.

Wonderful, Ross, he thought. Carrie would be so impressed with your juvenile behavior.

Mark broke eye contact first.

Ben ducked his head and rubbed his forehead to cover a grin of adolescent-grade triumph.

Lips pursed, Lana glanced back and forth between the two men, as if watching an invisible tennis match. Then she checked her watch and stood. "Oh . . . gotta scoot."

Ben turned away from Mark's scowl. "Me, too."

Having spent a good part of the day in Carrie's company, an evening alone held little appeal. But Ben was even less inclined to sit around shooting the breeze with Mark.

"Well, ta ta." Lana waggled her fingers at Mark

Calypso Wind 71

across the table. Then she leaned over and gave Ben a casual peck on the cheek that carried no deeper implications, and hurried off.

After Lana was gone, Mark and Ben parted company with somewhat more formality than the occasion warranted.

In no rush to be anywhere, Ben took the long way around, following the curving beachside walkway that led to the pool deck. The pool was empty. He moved through the wide doorway into the lobby.

The lobby teemed with guests clad in a brilliant array of peacock colors, heading out for a taste of the island's nightlife. Feeling more alone than ever, Ben worked his way against the flow of traffic toward the bank of elevators. An elevator arrived right in front of him, disgorging a chattering wad of tourists.

When they had walked past him, Ben stepped into the empty elevator. The door closed. His knuckle hovered briefly over the button for the third floor, then he punched the one below it with a vengeance.

Up on the second floor a moment later, he unlocked the door to his room and strolled through the sitting room to the bedroom. The balcony doors were open, the fading sunset casting the room in deepening shadows. He hit the light switch and went as still as stone.

Fists clenched at his sides, he surveyed the mess. A tangle of shirts and socks trailed from open drawers. The contents of the attaché case that he had left unlocked on the dresser were strewn across the bed, the case itself tossed to the floor. In the dressing alcove, the rest of his clothes lay scattered beneath their wooden hangers.

Ben's jaw clenched, then slid to one side. He scowled at his rifled belongings for several minutes before it occurred to him that he might have walked in on the intruder. He stole silently over to inspect the space on the far side of the bed. Then he crept around to the bathroom and eased the door wide open.

After assuring himself that no one was about to leap out at him, Ben made a conscious effort to relax the tension in his body. Once he had his temper in check, he moved resolutely to the nightstand.

A plastic-coated list of resort phone numbers was propped next to the phone. He had already punched in two numbers of the three-digit code for Calypso Beach Security when he paused to survey the room once more.

During his brief conversation with Lana Fuller a short while ago, Ben hadn't gotten the impression that the resort management hadn't pulled the plug on Galaxy Tours as a result of the earlier burglary. Not yet, anyway. But reporting one more intrusion, he figured, just might break the camel's back.

A big risk there. The conditions of Price Carmichael's will had stated very clearly that Carrie must in no way be tainted by scandal, however distantly. If Galaxy Tours got kicked out of Calypso Beach because one of its clients was a thief, Ben might as well fly back to Boston and feed the inheritance contract through the office shredder.

Besides, he couldn't see that he had much to gain by calling Resort Security to report this break-in. He had deposited all his valuables, including the Carmichael inheritance contract that Carrie had yet to sign, in the resort safe.

He took another moment to study the room carefully. As far as he could tell, the burglar hadn't damaged or made off with a thing. Fifteen minutes of straightening up, and all would be as it had been.

Not that Ben was kidding himself. But there were bigger fish to fry here, and this incident might have nothing to do with the series of burglaries that had plagued the resort. Unless he could come up with a connection, he simply couldn't risk this break-in being lumped in with the others.

Ben tapped the telephone receiver lightly against his chin, then carefully returned it to its cradle.

Chapter Six

The ancient bus rattled to a halt near the cluster of tourists waiting outside the front gate of the Calypso Beach Resort. Lolling behind the big steering wheel, the driver yawned widely as Carrie ushered a dozen Galaxy clients aboard. Each paused at the cigar box coin receptacle taped to the dashboard, struggling to puzzle out the various denominations of their Jamaican coins.

Carrie didn't try to rush them. That was what she loved most about the islands—no one was ever in a hurry. No one except the tourists.

"If we'd taken the resort shuttle instead of a public bus," Mark Hanes muttered, following her up the steps, "we'd be in Montego Bay by now."

"Right. And you would have missed all the fun of

getting there." Carrie wished Mark would loosen up and get into the spirit of the excursion.

"My treat." Mark reached over her shoulder and tossed the proper coins into the cigar box.

Leave it to an accountant to have the local monetary system down pat from the get-go, Carrie thought. She smiled her thanks, trying hard not to let her gaze drift up past his eyes. Just as she'd expected, Mark's hair color had come from a bottle, and exposure to the Jamaican sun had produced the usual results. His ash-blond hair hadn't exactly turned orange—not *exactly*. But it was getting there fast, making it difficult not to stare. And she didn't want to be rude.

Carrie felt ashamed of herself. Mark had been extremely kind since word of the latest room burglary had spread among the tour group. She wasn't sure if any clients, including Mark, had learned that the Calypso Beach management was trying its best to point the finger at Galaxy Tours. But she had a feeling that no matter what the resort chose to do, Mark would stick by her side. In the face of so much uncertainty, she was grateful for his loyalty.

Unfortunately, that was as far as her feelings for Mark went. When she was with the accountant, there was none of the jittery electricity that she had begun experiencing when she was anywhere near Ben Ross. Not even a tiny spark.

These past few days, Carrie had spent an astonishing amount of time trying to convince herself that she wasn't actually attracted to her late uncle's devilishly handsome attorney. And she had every reason to do so. After all, Ben Ross was pulling out all the stops in his attempt to manipulate her into signing the odious inheritance contract—something she had no intention of doing.

With a grinding of gears, the bus jolted forward as Sybil Rodgers waved to Carrie from her seat midway down the bus. Holding onto her wide-brimmed sunhat, Carrie eased along the narrow aisle toward her.

The seats were crowded mostly with locals. Tourists settled in here and there, notable for their flashy sneakers and digital cameras. Sybil had managed to save the entire bench seat in front of her, the only vacancy left on the bus.

"Take the window, Mark," Carrie said. "I've seen the scenery lots of times."

"Okay." Mark slid across the seat. "You get the window on the return trip."

Without warning, the driver stomped on the brakes. Thrown off balance, Carrie plopped down hard on the bare metal seat as a passenger bounded aboard at the last second. The bus started up a second time. Carrie resettled herself, smoothing the flowered skirt of her sundress. She was just removing her straw hat when the devil himself eased down onto the outside edge of the seat.

"Ben! What—"

"Isn't this great?" Ben glanced around at the other

passengers, grinning. "If this was Boston, the driver would have slammed the door in my face and kept right on going."

Carrie eyed the expensive brown-and-white dashiki he wore over crisp white jeans. She was finding it more and more difficult to picture him in a pinstripe suit. He turned his Huckleberry grin on her. She blinked, wondering why she found that narrow space between his front teeth so incredibly endearing.

"How's the bug bite?" Ben lifted her hat from her lap. Before she could stop him, he raised the hem of her dress a couple of inches to inspect the still-angry blister on the inside of her knee. "Jeez. Shouldn't you have a Band-Aid on that?"

She batted away his hand. "The tape won't stay stuck in the tropics."

"No kidding? Live and learn."

Ben reached an arm behind her to brace himself on the too-narrow seat, his thigh pressed firmly against hers. To Carrie's left, Mark stared grimly out the window. Awkwardly sandwiched between the two men, she stared straight ahead. With her arm pressed against Ben's ribcage, she could feel his heartbeat still racing from his sprint to catch the bus. Or was it her own pulse, running away with itself?

Something landed in Carrie's lap. She looked down at a cloth doll lying atop her straw hat. A pudgy toddler with shiny black cornrowed braids was in the process of clambering onto Ben's lap. Carrie watched, amused, as the bright-eyed tyke retrieved her doll, tucked a thumb into her mouth, and settled back against Ben's chest.

The bus hit a pothole and bounced. Ben clamped a hand around the child to keep her from tumbling into the aisle—the only indication that he was even aware of her presence. Carrie watched him gaze out through the far windows at a passing stretch of beach, the toddler nestled drowsily in his arms.

He's a magnet, she thought. *Birds, dogs and babies.* Something in Carrie stirred, but she refused to add herself to the list. Even so, if Ben had turned and looked at her then, she was pretty sure she couldn't have stopped herself from smiling.

"I'll carry that for you," Mark said.

Carrie tried to resist as they started down another row of open-air shops in the straw market. But Mark insisted on relieving her of her empty string shopping bag.

So far, she hadn't bought a thing. But Ben had closely watched her dickering with shopkeepers as he tried to get a feel for her negotiating skills—something she would need if she assumed management of the Carmichael estate. She had done all right with a cheap blue dashiki, though in the end she had decided not to buy the shirt. But now when she picked up a carved wooden head the size of a pepper grinder, he couldn't keep his mouth shut.

"You're joking," he said. "That isn't even stained

properly. Look, it's covered with cordovan shoe polish. In a dry climate, the wood will split wide open."

"It's a wonderful example of primitive art," she insisted. "Not to mention a product of the free enterprise system."

He took the carving from her and gave it a closer inspection. The carving was primitive, all right, and the shoe polish felt sticky in the heat. "You're really into supporting free enterprise, aren't you?"

"Sure. It's getting harder and harder for small entrepreneurs to get their dreams off the ground, especially here where import-export duties are so outrageous."

"I don't know." Mark shook his head, dabbing at his sweaty face with a handkerchief. "What's needed is some good old American get-up-and-go."

Carrie looked at him as if he had kicked the family dog, and took back her shopping bag. "Island culture is laid-back, Mark," she said. "In a tropical climate, it's suicidal to be otherwise. But that doesn't mean island people are lazy."

Mark started to interrupt, but she had a bee in her bonnet and wouldn't let him.

"The unemployed here aren't so different from back home or anywhere else," she said. "It comes down to a lack of opportunity and the unavailability of startup capital. You've got this big engine—people—and nothing to prime it with."

The accountant reddened beneath his sunburn, obviously taken aback by her nutshell lecture.

"I'm impressed, Carrie," Ben said, sensing that he had glimpsed just the tip of the iceberg, and that she had more than just a pedestrian grasp of basic business economics.

Carrie blushed. "I'm sorry, Mark, that was rude," she said, as if she hadn't heard Ben. "I didn't mean to jump up on a soapbox."

Mark let her off with an embarrassed shrug. Ben was disappointed. He wished Mark had stood up for his own opinion and forced Carrie into further rebuttal. He would like to have heard more from her on the subject. But at least the exchange had diverted her attention from the wood carving, which Ben discreetly returned to the shelf.

They rejoined the herd of tourists milling along the straw market's walkways. Sunlight filtered through Carrie's broad-brimmed hat, speckling her shaded face and shoulders. Her quick and passionate display of ideals had somehow deepened Ben's desire to touch her. The more he found out about Price Carmichael's niece, the more he wanted to know.

Minutes later, Ben put a hand on her arm, drawing a scowl from Mark. "Mmm. Where's that smell coming from?"

"Jerk chicken," Carrie murmured, sniffing the air and looking hungry. "Over there." She pointed toward the street, where savory smoke curled from beneath the lid of a cooker. Mark squinted at it skeptically.

Ben nudged Carrie. "How about it?"

Calypso Wind

She looked a little doubtful herself. "I don't know. I've never actually tried it."

Ben stepped back and gave her a look of exaggerated alarm. "How could you not have tried something that smells that good?"

Then it struck him: On Carrie's budget, souvenirs—even cheap ones—probably didn't fit. And suddenly, right there in the busy market, Ben was seized by a powerful desire to show her what she had been missing.

"Don't wander far," he said, taking her hand. "Promise?"

Carrie nodded. Mark glowered. Ben flashed the accountant a savage grin and took off through the mob toward the jerk chicken vendor.

As he paid for his purchase and waited for the spicy, piping-hot meat to be rolled into newspaper, the *bra-a-at* of a small engine drew Ben's attention across the street. Then his grin returned. Jerk chicken in hand, he trotted across the street.

Ten minutes later, he was back, straddling a rented moped, the paper-wrapped chicken balanced on one handlebar. Maneuvering the bike over the curb, occasionally revving the engine in warning, he eased through the sidewalk crowd toward where he had left Carrie.

He found her outside a shop where Mark had just bought himself a straw hat to cover his orange hair. With the engine idling quietly, Ben eased the moped up close behind them. When Carrie turned, he grinned at her, trying to ignore the fact that she was clutching a garish papier-mâché parrot.

Carrie gaped at him.

Mark snorted in disgust.

"Are you ready, Carrie?" Ben patted the narrow passenger seat behind him.

"For what?" she asked, hugging the parrot.

"Ready to get off the beaten path and feel the wind in your hair. To see and smell and taste new adventures in tropical paradise." He patted a wad of brochures tucked into a small rack on the handlebars. "Check out the local flora and fauna."

"I can't go gallivanting off, Ben. I have a tour group to—"

He laughed. "In case you haven't noticed, most of your group took off for the Parrot Patio a half hour ago to beat the noon rush. The rest are lined up over there at the bus stop, ready to head back to Calypso Beach. It's just you and me. And Mark."

Mark gave him a stony look as Carrie eyed the moped.

"Surely you don't expect me to abandon Mark," she said.

"Of course not. We can get Mark a bike, too." Ben leaned forward and peered closely at Mark's arms. "Although I'd think twice about it if I were you, buddy. Looks like you're developing a nasty case of sun poisoning there."

Mark looked at himself, startled. A thick red rash

Calypso Wind 83

covered the insides of his arms from his wrists to the sleeves of his polyester polo shirt.

Carrie joined the inspection. "Oh, my, he's right, Mark. You'd better get in out of the sun, or you'll be sick for the rest of your trip."

Mark scowled at the rash, as if suspecting that he was the victim of some kind of trick. "It doesn't even itch."

"Hey, I kid you not, friend." Ben shook his head. "You can't play around with sun poisoning. I once saw a guy in Barbados who swelled up like a blowfish. You could end up going home on a stretcher."

Mark paled beneath his sunburn, then glanced toward the corner where locals and tourists were climbing aboard the bus. "Well . . . maybe you're right," he said.

"Stop at the front gate and pick up some aloe vera from the Darnell kid," Ben said helpfully. "It'll help with the rash."

The accountant leveled a dark look at Ben, then trudged off toward the bus. As soon as Mark was gone, Ben looked at Carrie. She did not seem happy.

"That was rude, Ben."

"What?" He spread his free hand, all innocence. "You think I slipped the guy a sun poisoning pill or something?"

"We should go back with him."

"We?" He grinned. "Need I remind you that I'm not part of the tour? Besides, holding his hand won't help with that rash. He just needs to get in the shade and wait it out."

Ben waved the bundle of jerk chicken, wafting the spicy-smoked aroma her way. Carrie's lips parted. After a moment, the tiny frown line between her eyes faded. He watched her inhale deeply, then swallow.

She glanced one more time toward the bus stop, visibly waffling.

At last, just as Ben began to fear that he was losing her, she returned her attention to the moped. "Will that thing really carry both of us?"

The moped engine strained, whining like an enraged hornet as they sped along the straight, narrow road. Carrie kept her arms firmly locked around Ben. Every now and then, he reached back and touched her leg, as if to make sure she was secure. But she had never felt freer, with the wind whipping through her hair.

They had stopped alongside the road to eat the jerk chicken beneath a big pimento tree, taking their time while a steady shower of red-orange blossom petals drifted down from the branches high overhead. A few miles farther along, they had stopped again to quench their thirst at a roadside refreshment stand, where bees swarmed over the soft-drink taps.

"Unlike flies, honey bees don't leave germs—they take sweets," Ben had said. "Somewhere out there is a bee hive filled with cola-flavored honey."

Carrie had laughed, not sure if she believed him. It

Calypso Wind 85

didn't seem to matter. She was having too much fun. Remarkably, while in Ben's company she felt as if she were seeing the brilliant colors of the island and inhaling its rich fragrances for the first time.

She closed her eyes against the exhilarating wind, conscious of the tiny vibrations of the bike, and of the delicious warmth of the sun on her shoulders. She was still a little amazed that she had permitted Ben to practically shanghai her. She should be back at the resort, around in case Galaxy clients needed assistance. She should be checking to make sure Mark was staying out of the sun. She should be . . .

Ben covered her clasped hands with one of his.

Carrie's eyes popped open, every thought flying clear out of her mind. Realizing how close she was leaning against his broad back, she tried to unlock her hands and shift away. But Ben held on, pressing her hands firmly against his chest. They rode like that for another mile or so, across North Gully and Albion Road. She forced herself to breath shallowly, struggling to calm the pounding of her heart.

The engine pitch abruptly wound down. Ben released her hands and steered the moped off the road onto a flat parking area in front of a small clapboard building. When he killed the engine, Carrie leaned back, bumping against the papier-mâché parrot and her straw hat tied to the bracket behind the passenger seat.

She had seen the unhappy look Ben had given the parrot back at the straw market. She didn't have the nerve to explain to him that she had blown her meager budget on the gaudy bird because it reminded her of the hookbills at the Sand Dollar restaurant.

Assaulted by disconcerting visions of birds and dogs and babies clustered around Ben Ross, she turned her attention to the building.

"What is this place?" she asked.

"Some kind of store. Let's take a look."

"I don't know, Ben." She glanced at her watch. "Maybe we should get back to Calypso Beach. We've been gone a couple of hours now."

"Okay. But let's take a look inside here first."

Carrie slid off the passenger seat and shook out her skirt. Ben was looking at her, a slight smile playing at his lips. She felt herself blush, and wasn't sure why she suddenly felt so uncertain under his gaze. In desperation, she turned to study the building.

"There doesn't seem to be a sign," she said.

"That isn't unusual out in the countryside."

Ben strode to the open front door and peeked inside, then motioned her over. Carrie joined him.

The interior of the building consisted of a single small, low-ceilinged room. Rows of rough wooden shelves lined the two side walls, and a narrow plank table nearly filled the center of the cracked linoleum floor. A sparse assortment of canned foods occupied the shelves. A stack of red and yellow plastic buckets stood in one corner, along with the ever-present ice chest containing soft drinks and bottled water. Not enough capital, Carrie observed, to properly stock the all-purpose store that it aspired to be.

The table displayed a dozen or so bleached muslin blouses and aprons beneath a hand-lettered cardboard sign reading BUTTERFLY LADY. Carrie picked up an apron and carried it over to the sunlight trickling through the open doorway.

"Ben, this is gorgeous embroidery." Her fingertips glided over the tiny, delicate stitching.

He pulled a brochure from his hip pocket and flipped through the colorful pages of Jamaican fauna. Stepping closer, he compared the design on the apron with several of the illustrations.

"Looks like a life-size Giant Swallow Tail butterfly," he said. "According to this guide, it's found only in Jamaica."

"And it looks real enough to flutter away."

Ben moved back to the table and began sorting through the items. "Look here. The Jamaican national bird, a Streamer Tail Hummingbird. And a mongoose. A tree frog. An ackee plant, complete with fruits." He whistled softly. "Whoever did these is a real artist, and a naturalist."

Ben held up a blouse to show her the intricate leaf-covered branch stitched across the back. Joining him at the table, Carrie realized the branch wasn't covered with leaves after all.

"Zebra butterflies," he said. "They roost in swarms like this at night. I've seen them do that."

She set aside the apron and took the blouse from him, holding it up to herself. The butterflies wrapped around from the back, seeming to flit across her waist. A single perfect specimen rested over her heart.

"Who is this Butterfly Lady?" she wondered. "These should be sold in the best shops here on the island—and in the States—not stuck way out here on a back road."

He cocked his head and smiled at her. "You look good in butterflies."

Carrie's ears went hot. She quickly returned the blouse to the table.

"You should buy it," he said.

She laughed, jittery over the intense way he kept looking at her. "Not on my budget." She adored the blouse, but the papier-mâché parrot had already sent her budget into a tailspin. It didn't take much.

"But you could afford it," he said quietly, reaching out to stroke the design on the blouse without taking his gaze from her.

It all came back to that, she thought, knowing Ben was referring to the inheritance contract that he was still so determined to get her to sign.

Suddenly, her chest felt tight. They had been having so much fun the past couple of hours that Carrie had let herself forget Ben's primary mission. The shadow of Price Carmichael settled in between them.

Ben seemed to notice her abrupt change of mood, and his smile faded into a look of concern. Just as he

Calypso Wind 89

started to say something more, a horrendous sound of rending metal came from outside.

Carrie was startled motionless.

Squeezing past her, Ben bolted out the door. She raced out after him, choking as they were momentarily engulfed in a blinding cloud of dust. She heard rather than saw a vehicle roar off down the road.

As the dust slowly settled, Carrie stared in shock at the mangled moped, squashed nearly flat on the hard-packed dirt of the parking area. Her papier-mâché parrot lay shattered, one bright red eye staring in alarm from the wreckage.

She let out a strangled cry.

"Well . . . doesn't that beat all?" Ben's mild tone bewildered Carrie. He stared up the road for a moment, then walked over and lifted the moped onto its twisted wheels. The bike looked absurdly one-dimensional. He let it drop. "Looks like something out of a Roadrunner cartoon."

"This isn't funny, Ben!"

He glanced back at Carrie, then came over and grasped her shoulders.

Shaken, she wished he would take her in his arms. Instead, he touched her cheek with one thumb, so gently that it took her breath away. Then he leaned down and looked her in the face.

"Hey, nobody's laughing," he said. "But it isn't the end of the world. It's just a moped, not a Mercedes. Replacing it won't bankrupt me."

Her shoulders sagged.

Of course, he was right. Ben had worked for Price Carmichael—he still did. But she had never been in a position where a minor accident, not to mention a total wipeout such as this, wouldn't devastate her finances. And she could tell that was something Ben wanted her to see—that she didn't have to live on such a short shoestring.

Carrie wondered what it must be like to be financially secure. She could find out in a heartbeat just by signing her name on a dotted line. But she wasn't even tempted. She would rather have nothing than to feel bought, especially by the uncle who had turned his back on her and her mother.

She rested her head on his chest for a few seconds, suddenly lightheaded.

"How could this have happened?" she asked.

"Just some crazy hit-and-run driver."

They turned together and squinted off down the road in the direction in which the car had disappeared. After a moment, Ben put an arm around her. Carrie tilted back her head to look up at his face. After his marked lack of concern over the moped, she was startled to find him looking deeply worried.

Chapter Seven

Later that afternoon, Carrie lolled in a hammock chair with her feet buried to her ankles in warm sand. She watched another gentle wave wash up onto Calypso Beach, then resumed stroking the intricate butterfly pattern that wrapped around the front of her blouse.

Lana perched on a driftwood log nearby in the shade of a small grove of coconut palms. Located just outside the resort's beach boundary, the log served as an informal salon for tourists inclined to try out distinctive island coiffures.

Mark lay in a patch of deep shade nearby, glumly pretending to read a booklet on Jamaican history, though he hadn't turned a page in a good twenty minutes. Carrie had concluded that his mood bore little connection to the angry sun-poisoning rash that he had been forced to cover with long pants and a long-sleeve shirt.

"How did you and Ben get back here to the resort?" Lana asked, passing a white plastic bead over her shoulder to the woman who was deftly braiding them into her raven hair.

Carrie glanced at Mark. If Lana didn't stop bringing up Ben in front of him, she thought, the accountant was going to grind his teeth down to the gum line.

"We had to hike about a mile to a phone. The resort manager sent a car to pick us up."

Ben had apologized profusely for having left his cell phone back at the resort. But Carrie had actually enjoyed the hike once she got over the shock of the hit-and-run accident. With his pocket guides to the local flora and fauna, Ben had turned the trek into a pleasant nature walk.

After dropping Carrie off, Ben had prevailed upon the driver to take him back into Montego Bay so he could settle up with the moped owner. Carrie had insisted on paying her share, even though she knew she would be paying off the credit card debt for months or years to come. But Ben would have none of that. Standing toe-to-toe with him out at the front entrance to the resort, Carrie had discovered that Ben could be every bit as stubborn as she could.

"I still think I should have paid for part of that bike," she muttered.

"Why?" Lana raised an eyebrow at her, and rolled her eyes at Mark. "The way I heard it, the outing was all Ben's idea."

Mark made a brittle sound, like a boot heel grinding on gravel, and turned a page in his booklet with a sharp snap of paper.

Carrie let the subject drop. But the expense of the wrecked bike wasn't the only issue of the day that bothered her.

Two hours after her return to Calypso Beach, a package had been delivered to her room by the concierge. Inside was the beautiful butterfly blouse from the roadside shop. Obviously, Ben had bought it for her, though Carrie had no idea when or how he had managed that.

She had called his suite immediately to inform him that she couldn't possibly accept such a gift, but there was no answer. And then she noticed the handwritten note in the box.

Carrie,
This is to apologize for the way our outing turned out, and for your having to hike so far. The Butterfly Lady claims the wearer of this blouse will always have a free heart. I told her you already did. Thanks for a memorable morning.
Ben.

She had sat on the edge of her bed for a long time, rereading the note, wondering at it. She had never thought of herself as having a free heart. For some reason, finding out that Ben saw her in that way touched her deeply.

Even so, it had taken her quite awhile longer to make up her mind to accept the blouse. Finally deciding it would be rude to refuse Ben's thoughtful gesture, she had slipped it on. And through some crazy trick of her imagination, her heart actually had felt lighter, freer.

"All finished, miss," the woman standing behind Lana announced.

"My, this feels cool." Lana shook her head to make the beads rattle. "How do I look, folks?"

"Different," Carrie managed.

"Like Bo Derek in *10*, but with black hair." Mark boosted himself up onto the log.

Carrie smiled at him, relieved that he seemed to be coming out of his bad mood at last.

Lana was clearly pleased with the comparison to her favorite old movie. Carrie took another look at her and decided Mark's tongue-in-cheek comparison wasn't far off the mark.

"You ought to have your hair cornrowed, Carrie." Before Carrie could brush off the suggestion, Lana gasped and slid off the log, shading her eyes as she peered up the sun-baked shoreline toward Calypso Beach. "Is that who I think it is?"

"Who?" Carrie squinted into the lowering sun, scanning the scores of bathers. Most of the males were

Calypso Wind

accompanied by women. She quickly eliminated those, aware that Lana never stooped to poaching.

"The one lying on the orange hammock at the edge of the surf, jiggling his gorgeous body."

Carrie finally found him. "Is he having a seizure?"

"No, silly. Can't you see the headphones? He's listening to music." Lana pressed her palms together. "I saw him on a poster outside the lounge. He's performing right here at Calypso Beach this weekend. He's that gorgeous rock star everyone's so gaga over."

Lana couldn't quite recall the man's name, but Carrie noticed that didn't stop her from grabbing up her tote and slinking off across the beach toward the unsuspecting quarry.

Carrie watched, enthralled, as Lana waded into the ankle-deep surf and leaned against the foot of the hammock frame. The rock star stopped twitching and raised his mirrored sunglasses. Exactly three minutes later, by Carrie's watch, they were walking off together toward Winston Brown's portable refreshment cart near the end of the beach.

As the pair blended into the crowd, Carrie discovered that Mark was just as engrossed in watching them as she had been. A wistful expression further softened his even features. Wondering if Mark had developed a crush on Lana, too, she felt sorry for the lonely accountant.

* * *

The lobby was library-quiet, suspended in the brief late-afternoon lull as resort guests retired to their rooms to dress for the tropical nightlife. Carrie came in off the pool deck with Mark Hanes at her elbow, beginning to feel a little desperate. Mark had tried every ploy in the book to get her to have dinner with him, and simply would not take no for an answer.

If Carrie hadn't already had a firm policy against dating Galaxy clients, Mark's unrelenting attentions—coupled with his intermittent surly attitude—would have driven her to create one.

She didn't want to be rude. But the more Mark kept after her, the less he compared well with Ben.

For a moment, she considered the differences between the two men. Mark was a nice enough guy when he was in a good mood. On the other hand, she had never seen Ben in a surly mood, even when she repeatedly refused to sign that blasted inheritance contract. He was warm and exciting, and didn't crowd her.

And then, there were all those dogs and birds and babies who seemed to be attracted to Ben on pure instinct. You, too, kiddo, she thought. You, too.

"There's a great place just up the beach," Mark said. "You'll love it. It's called the Sand Dollar. . . ."

She sighed. Mark was right. The Sand Dollar was a great place, and she had loved it . . . with Ben Ross.

Images of their evening at the Sand Dollar made her pulse quicken. And the way Ben had looked after her when she'd been stung by the wasp. Fingering the embroidered butterflies on her blouse, Carrie could almost feel again the heady exhilaration of speeding along a country road on the moped with the wind in her hair, and Ben Ross's big, gentle hand covering hers.

She turned toward the elevator bank, hoping Mark couldn't see her blush. Hoping, as well, that Mark didn't intend to follow her all the way to her room.

Voices drew her attention past a seating arrangement in the center of the lobby. She spotted Lana over by the front desk, in what appeared to be a heated discussion with a burly man in a lime-green sports coat. Lana looked worried.

"Excuse me, Mark," Carrie said, detouring across the lobby.

As Carrie approached, she caught the gravely sound of the burly man's voice, and slowed. On several occasions during past visits, she had spoken on the phone with Henry Matalon, the director of resort security, but this was the first time she had actually seen him in person. Like all resorts, Calypso Beach management liked for its in-house security force to maintain a low profile.

Lana spotted Carrie, and reached out to take her hand. "This is Miss Washburn," she announced to Matalon. "In the flesh."

The way she said it gave Carrie the discomforting impression that the pair had been talking about her. But when Carrie gave the security officer a curious look, he eyed her with an inscrutable expression.

"What is it?" She had a sinking sensation in her

stomach, expecting to learn that there had been yet another burglary.

"This is just crazy." Lana squeezed Carrie's hand. "This . . . *gentleman* seems to believe that you've wired a large amount of money off the island. I keep telling him that you don't have money, period."

Carrie nodded, then shook her head, confused. "I don't understand . . ."

"Mr. Matalon," Lana put a razor-edge on the name, "is as much as accusing you of committing the burglaries."

"What?" Carrie's eyes went wide. For several seconds, she couldn't seem to get her breath. "But . . . but . . . I don't even jaywalk!"

"That's what I've been trying to—"

"Wait just one minute!" Mark shouldered in, glaring at Matalon. "Who do you think you are, throwing wild accusations at Miss Washburn?"

Mark's unexpected intervention startled Carrie. As he raised a hand and shook a finger in Matalon's face, she felt the encounter spinning rapidly out of control.

"Are you a client of Galaxy Tours, sir?" Matalon's gravely voice had gone icy.

"Yes, he is," Lana interjected. Moving quickly to defuse the situation, she tucked Mark's hand between both of hers while casting a meaningful glance at Carrie. "And he should be out enjoying himself. Come along, Mark, let's see if we can scare up some more aloe vera for your rash."

With effort, Lana managed to turn Mark around and

herd him away from the desk. He threw an irate backward glance at Matalon, but finally relented and allowed himself to be led off.

Feeling at once relieved and abandoned, Carrie watched Lana retreat across the lobby with her client. When she faced Matalon once again, she could tell that Mark's surprisingly confrontational display hadn't helped her cause one iota. The security officer stared after the departing pair, then returned his hooded gaze to Carrie.

She cleared her throat. "Mr. Matalon, I assure you, I know nothing about money being transferred off the island in my name."

"But the fact remains that such a transaction has taken place, Miss Washburn."

He waited, rocking lightly on his heels, as if expecting her to say something more. But words failed Carrie. This had to be a misunderstanding of some kind, but for the life of her she didn't understand how it could have happened. She didn't even know how to go about transferring money from one country to another.

At last, Matalon stepped back, offering a slight, surprisingly elegant bow for a man of his build. "I'll be in touch, Miss Washburn."

Then he, too, strode away, leaving Carrie alone by the marble-topped front desk.

She took a long, deep breath and let it out with a whoosh, trying to release some of the tension. It didn't help much. For the past several days, she had been worried sick that she would lose her job if Galaxy Tours was banned from the resort in the wake of continuing burglaries. But never in her wildest nightmares had she imagined that she might be suspected of those break-ins.

The thought made her shudder.

A hand slid into view on the front desk. Carrie half-turned, taking in the familiar brown-and-white dashiki. In the split second that it took for that to register, she no longer felt alone. For another instant, she wanted to lean her head against Ben's broad chest and shut out the world. But that wouldn't solve anything.

"What was that all about?" Ben asked, shifting his hand to her arm.

Carrie realized that he must have observed the encounter with Henry Matalon. Her knee-jerk reaction was one of embarrassment. She wanted to sweep the entire misunderstanding under the rug, but there didn't seem to be much point in that. If she couldn't trust a lawyer with the truth, whom could she trust?

"There have been a number of burglaries here at the resort," she said.

"I know."

"Well, there seems to be a rash of them every time Galaxy Tours stays here."

He winced. "I know."

"You do?"

Ben seemed amused by her look of surprise. "I go

out of my way to know everything I possibly can about you, Carrie."

The better to persuade me to sign that inheritance contract, she thought.

"Am I supposed to be flattered by that?" she asked.

He hesitated, apparently giving her flip question more consideration than she had expected.

"Putting myself in your shoes," he said, "I guess I'd be pretty annoyed if someone kept nosing around in my business."

His concession surprised her. She took another deep breath and let it out. The security director's accusation had left her off balance. She didn't really want to be annoyed at Ben. He might be looking after her late uncle's interests, but in his mind, that was the same as looking after hers, wasn't it?

"Look, Carrie." Ben spread his hand, palm up, in an open gesture. "I only wanted to help. It looked like a pretty upsetting situation brewing here."

Her shoulders sagged. "Well, it was," she said. "Mr. Matalon seems to be trying to point the finger at me for those burglaries. He says a large amount of money was wired off the island in my name. Of course, that's a stupid—"

Carrie cut herself off in mid-sentence as Ben slowly dragged a hand down his face.

"Oh, brother," he said. "I ought to strangle myself."

She blinked, puzzled by his reaction. "What?"

"My mistake, Carrie." Ben shook his head, then offered her a rueful smile. "I should have anticipated that Resort Security would be suspicious of that transfer."

"Transfer?" She still didn't get it.

"The preliminary check from Price Carmichael's estate," he said. "The one you left on the table at the Sand Dollar that first night. I did a little research and had it deposited in your bank account in Atlanta."

For what seemed like an incredibly long time, she couldn't utter a word. Not one faint sound. Her entire body felt paralyzed, the door to her mind double-bolted shut. Then the heat began to flow back in. As she felt it rise rapidly into her face, Ben took her arm and gently steered her across the lobby. She went along because she was still too stunned to resist.

Dusk was settling in as they stepped out onto the deserted pool deck. Ben led her all the way down to the sidewalk skirting the beach before she put on the brakes and jerked her arm free.

"Ben Ross, how could you do that?" she demanded. "How could you go messing around with my bank account?"

"Like I said, it was a mistake," he said quietly. They stood close, but not touching. For a moment, the only sound was the surf pounding onto the shore a dozen yards away. "Don't worry. I'll square it with Resort Security right away."

"That's not the point, Ben. How could you do that without telling me?"

He wiped a hand down his face again. Carrie had never seen him look so troubled. She had never felt so troubled herself. A lump rose in her throat. To her further distress, she realized her eyes were brimming.

"Oh, jeez, Carrie. Don't do that. Please."

She sniffed and turned away. He moved closer, a hand barely touching her hair. She hunched her shoulders, willing him not to touch her, fighting back the tears. This was so embarrassing, but she couldn't help it. Ben had gone behind her back. Just when she had begun to have real feelings for the man, she felt betrayed.

"I care about you, Carrie." His voice was soft, strained. "I care about how you have to struggle to keep your head above water. About how that strap on your sandal is just about to go. About how you're going to have trouble staying in school if you lose this job with Galaxy. I care about how much you're worrying—the way you bite the corner of your mouth when you're under stress. Price left everything to you—*everything*. It's all yours. There isn't one good reason in the world why you shouldn't have it."

"I don't *want* his money."

He sighed. "Obviously. So reverse the transfer. But think twice before you do it."

"Why?"

"Because with that money, you can leave your job right now. Then there'll be no risk to your reputation if Galaxy Tours gets booted out of the resort."

She gave an emphatic shake of her head. "I can't leave Lana like that. Not after all she's done for me. I wouldn't have gotten as far through school if it wasn't for her."

Carrie sniffled, wiped away a lone tear that had skidded down her cheek, then turned around. Ben's face was in shadows, the coral-and-yellow sunset spread out behind him like a warm aura. From the corner of her eye, she detected movement—a yellow dog trotting up the beach toward them.

"Look, Carrie," Ben said, opening and closing his fists at his sides. "I had your best interests at heart, but I can see now that I committed a blunder. It won't happen again. I promise. Can we just get past this?"

She took a shaky breath that settled her a little. She wanted to believe he really had begun to care about her—that he wasn't just looking out for the interests of the Carmichael estate. With that hope in mind, and with the yellow dog trotting ever closer as if drawn by an irresistible force, she gave in and nodded.

Ben raised both hands and grinned at the sky, as if his fondest dream had come true. She smiled, her lips trembling at the corners.

Suddenly, those big, warm hands were on her face, cupping her jaw as if she were a fragile china figurine. Ben gazed deeply into her eyes, his grin softening into a look of surprised wonderment. Slowly, he lowered his head until their lips barely brushed. Carrie gasped and put her hands lightly on his chest, where she felt his sharp intake of breath at her touch.

"Oh, Ben," she whispered as his lips closed over hers and his arms cautiously encircled her.

Their kiss deepened. His embrace tightened, pulling her closer, the nearby surf hammering in slow rhythm with Carrie's heartbeat. She breathed in an aroma of sweet tropical flowers, feeling disembodied, as if she were floating in the soft island breeze.

When their lips finally parted, they clung silently to each other for a few minutes. One of them was trembling—she couldn't quite tell if it was her or Ben. With her head pressed against Ben's chest, Carrie opened her eyes and gazed out at the sunset-gilded surf. The beach spun dizzily for several seconds, then stabilized.

After awhile, Ben cleared his throat. Carrie suddenly felt awkward, standing there in his gentle embrace. Awkward and confused.

Something bumped against her calf. Carrie looked down at a wagging yellow dog leaning against Ben's leg. Her sense of awkwardness evaporated, but not the confusion. The sense of being off balance returned in full force.

With her hand pressed to Ben's chest, she could feel his heartbeat, strong and steady and reassuring. The mutt thumped her leg with its tail while casting adoring looks up at Ben.

Carrie believed in dogs. Right at that moment, she believed that every twitch of the yellow dog's body language pointed toward Ben Ross being a good and decent man. And no doubt about it, she felt herself smile, she wouldn't mind exploring the magic of Ben's kiss once more.

But she couldn't seem to get past one simple fact—that he was on the island as Price Carmichael's lawyer.

Chapter Eight

Still straining for breath as he waded out of the surf, Ben leaned forward and knocked the heel of one hand against his head to clear his ears. His legs were rubbery, the long muscles burning. Having solid ground under his feet again came as a powerful relief.

As if his mind were programmed to, he paused at the edge of the water and squinted toward the pool deck to see if Carrie had returned from town yet. When he didn't find her among the lunch mob, he moved on to the refreshment cart parked beneath a palm tree at the end of the beach sidewalk.

Winston Brown greeted him with a grin. "Hey, mon! You made it back by yourself. The lifeguards, they were thinking maybe you take it in your head to swim all the way to Miami."

Ben laughed dryly at Winston's ribbing, as well as at his own stupidity. If he didn't stop woolgathering while swimming, he was going to have to stay out of the water altogether. This was the second time he had nearly drowned himself that week. On both occasions, he'd had Carrie Washburn on his mind.

He was pretty sure that wasn't going to change anytime soon.

Winston opened the lid on the cart's cooler and reached in for a liter bottle of spring water. "Here you go, Mr. Ross. On the house."

Ben seized the bottle and guzzled half the contents before stopping for a breath. He never ceased to be amazed at how thirsty a person could get while swimming in tropical waters. "I owe you one, Winston."

"No problem."

The rubberiness had left Ben's muscles, but now they were cramping up. He paced up the sidewalk, stopping to stretch every now and then. Returning to the cart, he noticed Winston's calculating expression and gave him a quizzical look.

"This ting you owe me," Winston said, leaning heavily on his beguilingly melodious accent. "Would it be a big ting or a small ting?"

Ben smiled down at his feet. "Depends on how much it's going to cost me."

"Nothing, mon. Not one thin American dime." Winston took Ben's empty bottle and tucked it into the

Calypso Wind 109

trash bag hanging from the back of the cart. "I've got this idea, you see—an enterprise sort of idea—and I could use some advice."

"No problem."

Winston grinned. He pulled out the cash drawer built into the side of the cart. He lifted the front of the currency tray and plucked out a well-worn digest-size catalog, which he handed to Ben with a flourish. Then Winston stepped back and watched him expectantly.

Ben dutifully leafed through the thin catalog, glancing at the four-color photos. He wasn't sure what was being asked of him.

"Where did you get this, Winston?"

"From Gordon Darnell's sister, Lucia. She found it in a wastebasket when she was cleaning a guest's room."

Ben glanced up the beach toward where Darnell's dilapidated glass-bottom boat usually road the surf. Apparently, Gordon was off with a customer. "You related to the Darnells?"

"No." Winston chuckled. "But sometimes it seems hard to find anyone who isn't."

"His family hustles, I'll give them that."

"Yes. I have in mind teaming up with Gordon in this little enterprise. What do you tink?"

Ben turned the catalog over and scanned the mail order form on the back, frowning. "I don't know, Winston. I somehow can't see Gordon Darnell selling expensive designer Italian shoes."

"No, no!" Winston snatched back the catalog. "This is just the idea behind our idea."

"Which is?"

"An exclusive boutique in New York . . . with a mail-order catalog."

"Oh? Selling what?"

"At first, top quality cottage industry products from Jamaica. Then, once it catches on, items from all over the Caribbean." Winston pulled a slip of paper from his pocket. "We've started a list. Hand-dyed batik-silk fabrics from a shop near Falmouth. Fine jewelry made with island gemstones from an artisan in Ocho Rios. Antique jars filled with allspice . . ."

"Whoa!" Ben waved him into silence. "I thought you said this was a *little* enterprise."

"But it is! A consortium of little enterprises, with Gordon serving as chief procurer of merchandise all over Jamaica."

"With you running the boutique."

"Exactly."

Ben was intrigued. Aware of the obstacles they would have to overcome, he also thought Winston's dream had little chance of getting off the ground.

"You said you needed advice," he said, knowing what they really needed was a miracle.

"Business advice." Winston nodded. "Someone to help us know what we need in the way of import licenses, permits and such."

"Plus a large chunk of startup capital."

"A moderate chunk, actually. You see, Mr. Ross, we can get agreements from the cottage industries on our list to provide their products on consignment—just until the boutique gets off the ground, of course. And my wife and kids could work in the store at first, once they pick up on the proper accent." Winston winked. "So costs will be fairly low."

"That's a different twist." Ben was impressed by the amount of careful thought Winston and his dreadlocked partner had put into their idea. "You might have something there."

"But the banks won't take a risk on us because we have no background in business." Winston spread both hands. "And we can't afford to hire an advisor."

Ben nodded. "The old catch-22."

"They don't understand that we aren't just a bunch of dreamers, Mr. Ross. We want to build a solid future for our families. My older daughter wants to be a teacher. And one of Gordon's brothers, Lester, wants to be a lawyer."

"No kidding?" Rubbing his chin, Ben decided he ought to take another look at the skinny kid hawking aloe vera at the front gate.

"We aren't looking for a handout," Winston said. "We're looking for a hand up."

Ben was beginning to get a glimpse of what Carrie saw in people like Gordon and Lester and Winston—

their dreams. It had been a long time since he'd reminded himself that almost every major industry in the world had started out as someone's small dream.

Head down, he took a slow stroll back up the sidewalk while taking a critical look at his own history. Considering his background, Ben had been incredibly lucky to have stumbled onto such a powerful mentor in Price Carmichael. In all the years he'd worked for Price, he had kept his gaze focused tightly on the prize, never taking the time to look back down at the bottom of the ladder. And the higher he had climbed, he realized now, the lonelier it had gotten. With Price gone, it was lonely indeed.

He stopped and stared into the distance, forcing himself to remember just what his life had been like before the gold watches and hand-tailored suits. Back when he had been scratching and clawing for a toehold just like Winston and Gordon.

Returning decisively to the cart, he said, "Got a pen, Winston?"

Winston hurriedly dug into the cash drawer for a ballpoint pen and tore the back from a receipt book. Ben jotted down the phone number and address of his office. As an afterthought, he added his personal E-mail address and home phone.

"Next time you're in the States, bring me every scrap of information you have on your—" Ben arched a brow "—little enterprise. I'll help you draw up a business plan, which should help you persuade some financial institution to provide you with standing room on the bottom rung."

"But we can't afford—"

"Don't sweat that. If your boutique gets off the ground, you can give me a discount."

Looking slightly dazed, Winston gave him an exuberant two-fisted handshake. "I promise you, Mr. Ross, you won't regret this."

Ben turned and walked away, flexing his right hand, a lopsided smile twitching his lips. A dozen yards down the sidewalk, he did an abrupt about-face and retraced his steps.

"Say, Winston, I came across some embroidery yesterday that blew my—"

"The Butterfly Lady." Winston waved his list of cottage industries. "Miss Washburn showed me the blouse you gave her. Remarkable workmanship."

"Oh." The mention of Carrie's name startled him.

After the disaster the moped excursion had turned into yesterday, followed by his shortsighted stupidity in upsetting Carrie with the wire transfer, Ben had been more than pleased to see her wearing the blouse. Then those blasted tears had welled in her eyes—tears that were his fault. Before he had known what was happening, he was touching her face, his fingers in her mane of honey-colored hair, and she had let him kiss her not ten feet from where he now stood.

Still more amazing, she had kissed him back.

But kiss or no kiss, the last thing Ben had expected

was that Carrie Washburn would be out broadcasting that he—Price Carmichael's attorney—had given her the butterfly blouse.

Lost in thought, he smiled to himself. In some peculiar way, offering Winston Brown a helping hand had made him feel closer to Carrie. Ben realized that something inside him felt as if it were changing, evolving, and opening up.

He was still examining that intriguing bit of insight when he spotted a barefoot toddler with a yellow duckhead flotation device around his pudgy chest waddling up the sidewalk in his direction. Ben held his ground for a moment, waiting for the sprout to veer safely to the right or left. Instead, it steamed straight ahead, wedging the inflated duck between his knees and clamping both sand-speckled arms around his legs.

The public bus from Montego Bay clattered to a halt outside the main gate to the Calypso Beach Resort. The driver set the hand brake and turned in his seat to watch Carrie wheel a flashy new blue-and-red mountain bike down the narrow center aisle. Behind her, passengers scrambled to shift seats so they could see out the open windows on the left side of the bus.

At the front door, Carrie skipped down the steps. The driver handed the bike out to her before he, too, turned to peer out the window on the resort side of the bus. Carrie paused to gain control of her excitement, then wheeled the bike around the vehicle toward the gate.

Lester squatted at his usual spot beside a mound of succulent aloe vera leaves. When he saw her pushing the bike toward him, he stood, his eyes widening with interest.

She turned the bike sideways in front of him and lowered the kickstand. "Happy birthday, Lester."

He gaped at her, then at the bike. For the first time in the two years that Carrie had known him, Lester stumbled over his own tongue.

"But . . . this . . . this isn't my day . . . my birthday."

Carrie bent over and planted a resounding kiss on his cheek. "Then this is for all the ones I've missed. And it isn't just from me, Lester. It's from all the Galaxy Tours' guests—every single one of them—in gratitude for keeping them supplied with aloe vera."

She had taken up a collection.

Lester's eyes glazed. He reached out and touched the bike with such awe that her heart ached.

"It is all right?" she asked, thinking maybe she should have gone with the purple bike.

"Oh, Miss Washburn." He moved closer and wrapped his hands around the red handlebar grips, at last claiming the bike as his. "It is magnificent!"

He suddenly whirled and threw his arms around her. Carrie's eyes brimmed as the bus erupted with hoots and applause. If possible, she felt every bit as happy as the boy.

As the excitement died down, the bus rattled off down the road with a clashing and grinding of gears.

Carrie stood in the cloud of dust, watching Lester climb aboard his new bike and make big wobbly loops around the broad paved driveway. On the third loop, he glanced over at his box of aloe vera leaves. She could almost see his nimble mind working out a fresh set of possibilities.

Carrie smiled. She didn't really think of the bike as a gift. In Lester's industrious hands, it was more like an investment.

With a parting wave, she walked on up the long driveway toward the resort's lobby entrance. A small knot of curious employees and guests had gathered on the steps, apparently drawn by the commotion down by the highway. Carrie bit her lip when she spotted Ben among them.

By the time she reached the entrance, the group had broken up and gone back inside. Ben stood alone with his hands in the pockets of his shorts, waiting. She couldn't deny the rush of delightful sensations she experienced as he waited for her.

"What was that about?" he asked.

"Just a small celebration. The Galaxy clients chipped in and bought Lester Darnell a bike."

"Really? What's the occasion?"

Carrie shrugged. "Call it an investment in Lester's future. With the bike, he'll be able to double or triple his aloe vera sales territory, and his income."

Something flitted across Ben's expression, gone before she could decipher it. Had it been a smirk? She planted her hands on her hips. "Mind telling me what's so funny?"

"Nothing. I was just thinking the bottom rung is getting pretty crowded."

"Bottom rung? What are you talking about?"

He grinned. Then laughed outright.

Carrie's gaze fixated on the narrow space between his front teeth. The awkwardness that she had felt following their kiss yesterday returned. She tried to ignore the nervous flutter in her stomach.

Ben held out a hand. "Come on. Let's talk."

She checked her watch. "I have to lead a group over to Rose Hall for a tour of the Great House in an hour."

"This won't take long."

As he escorted Carrie inside, she was aware of how effortlessly he adjusted his much longer stride to match hers so they moved almost in lockstep. Oddly enough, walking beside him helped to relax the tension that had built up while they were outside. As they crossed the lobby and entered the lounge, she didn't object when he took her hand under the pretext of leading her to a table.

They found a quiet booth in a corner. After the bright sunlight, the lounge seemed darker and more secluded than it actually was. They ordered iced tea. Carrie munched on a bowl of pretzels until they were served.

Ben remained unusually quiet while waiting for their drinks. Then he took a long drink from his glass and grinned at her again.

"Looks like you helped to make Lester pretty happy," he said.

Carrie sipped her tea, replaying her own pleasure in her mind. "That's the best part of life, Ben. Bringing joy to other people. Helping dreams come true."

Moving in slow motion, Ben leaned forward and placed his elbows on the table, frowning in thought as if she had presented him with some novel, unexplored concept. That surprised Carrie. She wondered how much joy Ben Ross's money had brought him over the years.

"When you get right down to it, Ben, I guess that's what it's all about. And why I'll never sign that inheritance contract."

His gaze snapped to her face.

"Uncle Price didn't believe in other people's dreams," she said. "Least of all mine. I couldn't possibly take the money and name of a man like that. It would be like he bought me."

Ben frowned. Carrie could imagine how frustrating it must be for a man who was accustomed to boardroom legal maneuverings to be thwarted by a lowly travel agency tourguide. She wasn't expecting what he said next.

"Carrie, if there's one thing I've learned this week, it's the value of keeping an open mind." He folded his hands and rested his chin on his thumbs, studying her across the table. "I have to tell you something. While you were off shopping for Lester's new wheels, I was giving Winston Brown my home phone number. Free legal advice, and all that."

She put down her glass. "You jest."

"Nope. You've thoroughly tainted me." He appeared to find that as wondrous as Carrie did. "And that's only the beginning. You see, I have a sneaking suspicion that I'll be eternally grateful to you. Offering to help Winston with his grand scheme made me feel good. Better than I have in ages."

Carrie didn't know what to say.

With a chuckle, Ben helped her out. "I know. It's hard for you to stomach that you might share a small patch of common ground with a turkey."

"Ben, I have never called you a turkey."

"Maybe not. But if you go swearing that you've never thought it, you're liable to grow a very long nose."

She grimaced, drawing another chuckle. There was no point in denying that he was right.

"But you're wrong about one thing, Ben. I don't mind sharing common ground with you."

His gaze searched hers for a moment, then he reached out and covered her hand with his. "Hold that thought, Miss Washburn."

A jittery rush of warmth coursed through Carrie. Her fingers automatically entwined with his, and she felt an emotional connection between them quicken like a second heartbeat. But despite these thrilling physical sensations, when she looked across the table at Ben, he appeared strangely distant to her, as if she were seeing him through the ghost of Price Carmichael.

Chapter Nine

"Good grief, Lana," Carrie protested through the changing-room curtain. "I do have my reputation to uphold."

"That's what I'm getting at, sweetie. If you're not careful, you'll develop a reputation as a wallflower."

Carrie took a second look at the scrap of blue silk Lana had tossed to her over the curtain rod. It looked more like a slinky little tunic than an evening dress. She had never worn anything like it in her life, and couldn't see herself in it now.

"Lana, I could undergo open-heart surgery in this thing without even taking it off. Besides, the price tag is bigger than the dress."

"It's my money that I'm loaning you, silly. Go for it. Besides, the dinner party is tonight, and you're running out of time." After a pause, Lana added, "I don't hear the rustle of fabric in there."

With a sigh, Carrie relented. She had already tried on everything else in the store. She was beginning to regret having accepted Ben's invitation to dinner with Sam and Trish Rivers. Overnight, the intimate dinner had turned into a snazzy dinner party, and she suddenly felt as if she were in over her head.

The shimmering silk slid over her body like a cool breath of air. She smoothed it into place, relieved to discover that it wasn't nearly as revealing as she had expected. Then she turned to look at herself in the mirror.

"Speak to me, Carrie."

"I think it, uh, fits."

"Let me see." The curtain rustled and Lana leaned into the cubicle. They both stared at Carrie's reflection in the mirror for a long moment. Then Lana laughed. "Sweetie, if that dress fit any better, it would be against the law."

"You don't think it's too—"

"Oh, for heaven's sake," Lana said. "It comes nearly to your knees, and that mock turtleneck makes it look downright prim."

"From the front. What about . . . ?" Carrie turned to reveal her bare shoulder blades.

"I've seen more skin than that on a tennis court."

Carrie made a face at her. But when Lana ducked back outside, she took another look at herself. She

Calypso Wind 123

stood on tiptoe to simulate high heels, and fluffed at her hair. She had never even tried on a genuine evening dress before, and it felt like rich milk chocolate tasted—delicious.

"Thanks for floating me a loan, Lana," she said through the curtain. "And for helping me shop. I wouldn't have known where to begin." When she accepted the invitation from Ben, she hadn't even considered the fact that she didn't have a thing to wear to dinner at a famous actor's estate, never mind to a full-blown dinner party.

"Hey, it isn't every day that a girl gets to mingle with the filthy rich and notorious," Lana said.

Carrie suddenly went still, her gaze losing focus. All along, she had been a bundle of nerves over the prospect of meeting *the* Sam Rivers. But now it finally sunk in that what she was really looking forward to was spending the evening with Ben.

In this dress she thought. *With my hair up . . . like someone special.*

She hugged herself and whirled on one foot, smiling dreamily. Maybe there would be dancing. She imagined herself drifting along in Ben's arms to a soft island melody.

And that stopped her cold.

"Uh-oh. Lana?"

"What is it, Cinderella?"

"I don't know how to dance."

"Oh, for heaven's sake."

Minutes later, the street door opened. Sybil Rodgers strolled into the shop lugging a huge plastic shopping bag. Her face lit up when she spotted Lana and Carrie standing at the cash register.

"And here I was, feeling blue because I've been rattling around Montego Bay all by myself this morning," Sybil said.

Carrie glanced past her. "Arnold isn't with you?"

"Oh, the poor dear got carried away with all those luscious tropical fruits that are served up morning, noon and night. I'm afraid he's back in our room swabbing calamine lotion on a positively wicked case of hives." Sybil put down her bulging shopping bag. "I offered to stay with him, but Arnie insisted that I come on into town as planned. We still have four more grandkids to shop for."

Hives. Carrie made sympathetic sounds, thinking, It's always something.

Arnold and Sybil Rodgers were the most unlucky tourists she had ever met. If they weren't running afoul of the local flora and fauna, they were missing excursion buses or falling victim to a seemingly endless variety of petty maladies. She had to admire them for not letting it get them down.

The three of them watched the store clerk layer the evening dress with peach-colored tissue paper and carefully fold it into a box. Carrie had to glance away, already suffering a serious case of buyer's remorse. How was she ever going to repay Lana? And they hadn't even found shoes yet. And Lana had said something about suitable lingerie.

"What a gorgeous garment, Lana!" Sybil said.

"Don't look at me." Lana waggled her fingers at Carrie. "The dress belongs to her."

"You don't say." Sybil looked at Carrie with intense interest, as if matching her with such an elegant piece of fabric were a novel concept indeed. "You must be getting togged out for an event."

"That's the understatement of the year." Lana leaned close to Sybil and lowered her voice, as if divulging a state secret. "A gentleman friend is taking her to a dinner party out near Half Moon Bay tonight. Our little Carrie is going to wine and dine with Sam Rivers."

Standing a little apart, Carrie felt herself blush from head to toe as the two women chatted on about her as if she weren't there. The clerk handed her the garment box. The dress was so feathery-light that the box felt empty.

"Tonight, you say?" Sybil asked finally.

"That's right."

"Well, my word."

The blue silk evening dress didn't look like it belonged there, draped on its plastic hanger in Carrie's closet alcove. Neither did the new thin-strapped slingback heels lined up on the alcove floor. And certainly not the lacey undies that Lana had insisted that she buy, declaring that combining cotton underwear with a silk dress was nothing short of a sacrilege.

Carrie held the sales receipts for the shopping spree fanned out like cards. Their totals were almost enough to make her weep. She couldn't believe she had stood by and permitted Lana to talk her into spending so much on herself. The dress shop tab alone was enough to make her want to take everything back and call the whole thing off.

Almost.

The thought of meeting Sam Rivers wasn't what held her back. What kept Carrie on track for the evening was the thought of Ben Ross seeing her in that dress.

When a knock came on her door, she assumed it was Lana coming as promised to indoctrinate her on the mysteries of makeup. Carrie tucked the receipts into her overnight bag before opening the door.

Ben stood in the hallway in swimtrunks, a thick beach towel thrown around his neck. His hair was slightly windblown, but she could tell he hadn't been in the water yet. Instead of smelling like sunscreen and the sea, he carried a faint aroma of spicy aftershave. He grinned at her look of surprise.

"In the interest of free enterprise," he announced, "I've engaged Gordon Darnell's glass-bottom boat. Change into beachwear. I'll meet you at his skiff in ten minutes."

"What?"

"Lunch, Carrie. On a quiet beach. The kitchen is scaring up a picnic basket as we stand here dawdling. Let's shake a leg before Darnell's boat sinks."

Ben was gone before Carrie had a chance to object.

*   *   *

The outing took closer to half an hour to launch. Perched near the bow, Carrie gripped the straps on her lifejacket and peered down through the boat's clouded glass bottom at the sea floor. But they were moving too fast for her to catch more than fleeting glimpses of sea life.

Gordon manned the tiller of the antiquated outboard motor, his dreadlocks flying as the boat skimmed along the shallow waters of the coastline at full throttle. Ben sat in the middle, staring at the inch or so of water sloshing around his feet. Not that they were in any real danger of sinking—not with the shoreline within wading distance. Ben had made sure of that before allowing Carrie aboard.

With the day's fee, Ben thought, maybe Gordon could afford some much-needed paint and caulking.

Twenty minutes up the coast from Calypso Beach, the throaty whine of the outboard abruptly changed pitch as they rounded a sandy point dotted with palm trees. With an expert twist of the tiller, Gordon steered the boat past a patch of coral toward a secluded crescent-shaped beach.

While the motor idled, Ben hopped out into waist-deep water.

After making sure Carrie had a firm grip on the tote bag containing their lunch, Ben lifted her out of the bow. She laughed at his gallantry, and hung on tight around his neck. As he waded ashore with Carrie in his arms, the outboard sputtered, coughed, and roared back to full volume.

She looked over Ben's shoulder at the departing boat. "Shouldn't we have told Gordon when to pick us up?"

"That's all been arranged."

"Really?" She leaned back in his arms so she could see his face. "I'm impressed with your competence."

He grinned. "It's nice to know something about me impresses you."

She gave him a wry, sidelong look as he put her down on the beach. They both took a moment to survey their picnic site.

"Gorgeous," she said. "How did you find out about this place?"

"I didn't. I asked Gordon to use his imagination. Competent people know how to delegate."

"I see." Carrie lowered the tote to the dry sand just above the waterline.

Ben helped her unfasten the straps on the lifejacket and slip the apparatus off over her head. She had a Galaxy Tours T-shirt on over her bathing suit. She kept the T-shirt on. He couldn't help taking that as part of the veneer of reserve that she maintained where he was concerned.

He had kissed her once, and she had definitely kissed him back. They were more than a little attracted to each other. But apparently she still had trouble making the separation between him and Price Carmichael.

How ironic, Ben thought, that the very person who had brought them together now stood between them.

"Care for a swim?" he asked quietly.

"The food . . ."

With a playful growl, Ben dropped his wristwatch into the tote bag, grabbed Carrie's hand, and ran with her toward the water. She gave a startled yelp that tumbled into a birdsong of laughter. When he released her, she took three more strides on her own and dove gracefully into the surf.

They swam side by side, stroke for stroke, Carrie as sleek as a dolphin. A dozen or so yards out from the shore, Ben watched with pleasure as she suddenly jackknifed and disappeared beneath the waves.

Following her down into the sparkling blue waters, he put out a hand and felt the smooth shape of her ankle slide across his palm. She turned to look at him, tiny bubbles escaping her smile. Ben plucked a seashell from the sandy seabed and handed it to her. She found one for him. Then they shot to the surface, filled their lungs and dove again.

When they finally waded ashore some time later, Ben felt winded and sublimely happy.

He spread his beach towel on the warm sand. The single towel that he had brought along was inadequate for a two-person seating arrangement, which suited Ben just fine. He used that as an excuse to sit close to her, their arms and legs brushing.

"I'm starved," Carrie said, taking the words right out of his mouth.

As soon as they caught their breath, they pounced on the insulated food keeper in the tote bag, devouring peeled oranges, seasoned corn cakes and juicy slices of jerk pork.

Carrie watched Ben uncap a wide-mouth vacuum bottle and pour the contents into the lid. "What are those?" she asked.

"Frozen sliced bananas in rum-chocolate sauce." He speared a slice with a plastic toothpick, swirled it in the sauce and popped it into her mouth. "I bribed the chef."

"Mmm . . . remind me to marry the guy."

Ben fed her more slices, then tried the last one himself. It slid down his throat like a tiny, sinfully-rich glacier, in dramatic contrast to the blistering heat of the sun on his back. When the dessert was gone, they stretched out on the sand in the shifting shade of a palm tree.

Carrie closed her eyes against the brilliant sunlight reflected off the beach. Ben seized the opportunity to admire the slender, liquid lines of her body. Pale sand stuck to her glistening skin like a thin dusting of confectioner's sugar. Just lying there near her felt so peaceful.

Peaceful. The word reverberated through his mind, strange and new. He sighed contentedly, thinking this couldn't be real. Life was way too complicated for happiness to be this simple.

"You swim like a dolphin," he said.

"Oh, nice." Her eyes remained closed. "A dolphin is a small whale."

He smiled ruefully. "Okay, a tuna—the Maserati of the sea."

"Ick. Tuna are shaped like bombs."

Ben flicked sand at her leg. "Keep it up and I'll settle on barracuda."

Her lower lip pouted playfully. He wanted to lean over and kiss her, but knew that would be a mistake. When he had come up with the plan for this outing, his intent had seemed so perfectly clear to him: if he got Carrie completely alone without distractions, maybe she would listen to reason. But now reason seemed to be changing its spots.

Just being there with Carrie Washburn seemed as important to him as getting her signature on the inheritance contract.

Common sense told him that he couldn't have both.

Rolling onto his back, he stared up at the cloudless sky. No, he couldn't have both. And for the first time since the day Price Carmichael had walked into his life, Ben resented his mentor.

He was still examining that remarkably disturbing epiphany when the distant, thready sound of an outboard motor rose above the rhythmic whisper of surf rolling onto the beach. Carrie noticed, too. They sat up and shaded their eyes, squinting toward the tree-lined point that jutted into the sea.

Seconds later, a boat appeared, moving fast, its bow riding high out of the water. Even before it made a tight turn past the bed of coral and headed in toward the beach, Ben recognized Gordon Darnell in the stern.

Without taking her gaze off the boat, Carrie rose and brushed sand from her legs. "Gordon looks upset."

"Well, he can join the club." Ben didn't bother rummaging around in the tote bag for his Rolex. He hadn't even gotten around to talking with Carrie yet, not seriously. "He's a good hour early."

"Early?" Carrie glanced over at him. "I've never known Gordon to be in a hurry."

Just as Gordon appeared to be bent on running the boat right up onto the beach, he cut the motor and shoved the tiller hard to port. The boat swung around sharply, leaving the craft wallowing in shallow water broadside to the beach.

"You best come back now," Gordon shouted. "A bad ting is happening at Calypso Beach."

"Such as?" Ben called back from the water's edge. He was thinking the problem had better be along the lines of a category-five hurricane, or Darnell was going to have one irate customer.

"Another burglary, mon." Gordon stood up and waved them urgently toward the boat. "The management is very angry."

Ben's temper couldn't have cooled faster if he had taken a plunge into ice water. He remained perfectly still for several seconds, waiting for the debris from Darnell's bombshell to settle.

The danger of Carrie being trapped in a quagmire of scandal that wasn't of her making had just loomed immeasurably closer. He could just imagine the headlines if the supermarket tabloids got hold of this.

RAGS-TO-RICHES BOSTON HEIRESS LINKED TO RESORT THEFTS!

Once that dye was cast, the conditions of the inheritance contract would be officially violated. Then it would no longer be within Ben's power to complete his duty to fulfill Price Carmichael's last wishes.

As bad as that prospect might be, the inheritance itself had taken on a secondary importance in Ben's mind. He wasn't about to stand by and let Carrie be put through the wringer of an undeserved scandal. Not without a fight.

By the time he waded out and lifted Carrie into the boat, he was already thinking furiously about damage control.

A long shower and two aspirins hadn't made a dent in Carrie's headache. She put down the blow-dryer and scuffed out of the bathroom, flirting with depression. The news that Calypso Beach management had given Lana forty-eight hours to clear Galaxy Tours out of the resort was devastating.

She should have seen it coming. She *had* seen it

coming. But she hadn't really, truly believed it would happen until the brick wall actually fell on top of her.

Lana was in her room down the hallway, frantically working her phone, trying to find alternative accommodations for the tour group. That wouldn't be easy at the height of tourist season. At best, Galaxy clients would end up scattered in several resorts, presenting a logistical nightmare.

Carrie had offered to help with the phoning, but Lana had insisted that she go on to the dinner party at the Rivers' estate that evening as if nothing were amiss. The clients were not to be told a word about their upcoming eviction until new arrangements could be worked out—assuming that was possible.

Of course, Lana was right about there being no point in upsetting everybody any more than necessary. But for Carrie to just go on to the dinner party didn't seem right.

She sagged onto the corner of her bed, still tempted to call Ben and beg out of the evening. Then again, that might be rude at this late hour.

She and Lana already were indebted to Ben for his unsolicited backing during the brief but painful scene in the resort manager's office earlier in the afternoon. Ben had somehow succeeded in cutting an impressive professional figure while standing there in damp swimtrunks and tousled hair. The manager had seemed somewhat intimidated by Ben's legal jargon. Best of all, he had persuaded the manager to keep a lid on the eviction notice at least until tomorrow.

But a disaster delayed was a disaster all the same.

With a disconsolate groan, Carrie slid off the bed and knelt beside the tote bag that had contained their picnic lunch. She opened the bag and began stacking empty food containers on the floor for room service to pick up later. The vacuum jar gave her pause. She closed her eyes for a moment, recalling how Ben had fed her the chocolate-covered frozen banana one delectable slice at a time.

Groping around at the bottom of the bag, she came up with Ben's watch. With all the excitement, he had forgotten to retrieve it when they returned to the resort. Just holding something that belonged to him was somehow comforting. Fingering the gold case, Carrie felt the engraving on the back. She turned it over and held it up to the light.

Ben—My Designated Son—P.C.

She stared at the inscription for a very long time before placing the expensive watch back inside the bag out of her sight.

Lana strode out through the lobby's beachside doorway wearing a tropical-print sundress and the brightest smile she could muster. Scanning the crowded deck and pool, she spotted only a handful of her tour clients. Among them, Arnold and Sybil Rodgers splashed waist-deep in the shallow end of the pool, sporting coordinated salmon-and-white swimwear.

For the moment, Lana scrupulously avoided that end of the pool. After three harried hours on the phone, she had finally—miraculously—managed to negotiate accommodations for her clients at a resort five miles farther along the coast. The new accommodations were of only slightly lower quality than Calypso Beach. Most of her clients probably wouldn't even notice the difference.

Even so, the crisis had left her too drained for chitchat. What she needed right now was some fresh air and . . .

Mark Hanes popped into Lana's line of sight, waving at her from a small table on the far side of the pool. She kept looking around, trying to pretend that she hadn't noticed him. But he kept semaphoring both arms, signaling for her to join him. With a sigh, she gave in and headed his way.

"You look in need of refreshment." Mark held out a chair for her, then made an adjustment in the table's striped umbrella. "Sit tight. I'll be right back."

Lana watched Mark hurry off into the crowd. He returned a few minutes later with tall, frothy drinks topped with paper parasols.

"You are one sweet fella," she said, accepting her glass.

"Anything for a beautiful lady."

He pulled his chair around so both of them sat with

their backs to the pool. They sipped their drinks quietly, gazing out at sailboarders skimming back and forth across the sun-dappled waves beyond the surf line. Never one to worry unnecessarily, Lana worked hard at putting the upcoming eviction out of her mind for the moment.

After awhile, she relaxed.

It didn't last long.

Mark scooted his chair closer. In an undertone that didn't carry beyond their table, he said, "I heard about the latest break-in. I guess there's no hope of keeping this one swept under the rug."

His words fell like stones into the pit of Lana's stomach. She turned slowly and looked at him. With a sad, sympathetic smile, Mark reached over and patted her hand.

"How did you find out?" Lana asked, almost afraid to hear his answer. She had been counting on a day's breathing space before having to deal with the inevitable chaos of alarmed clients.

"Oh, I stopped by the resort office to send a fax." He shrugged. "Overheard the head of security talking with the manager."

Lana's shoulders sagged.

"Now take it easy," he added hurriedly. "The word isn't out quite yet, and my lips are sealed."

Mark hadn't mentioned the pending eviction, Lana noticed, so at least she had the timing of that information release still under control. Her clients, including

Mark, would get the unsettling news first thing in the morning.

She had given the other resort a song and dance about why Galaxy Tours was switching accommodations. But once the grace period that Ben Ross had negotiated expired, the news that her group had been evicted by Calypso Beach would spread like wildfire along the island's resort grapevine. After that, Galaxy Tours would be about as welcome as a gang of Barbary pirates throughout Jamaica's tourist industry.

She smiled bravely at Mark, but deep down Lana wanted to cry.

"I'm sure the culprit will be caught," she said. "It's just a matter of time."

"Oh, absolutely." Mark glanced around, then cupped a hand over his mouth. "But who do you think it is?"

"Not one clue."

"Well, I have my suspicions."

"And who would that be?" Lana had to struggle to keep an edge out of her tone. She really didn't want to be having this conversation, especially with one of her own clients.

He hesitated. "Well, to be perfectly honest, I've never liked the look of that shyster lawyer who's been hanging around Miss Washburn."

Lana gave him an incredulous look. "Ben Ross? You can't be serious."

"Why not? I've done some asking around, and it turns out he comes down here to Jamaica fairly regularly. And he's stayed at Calypso Beach at least twice before."

"That doesn't make Ben a thief, Mark."

He held up a hand, as if to stop her from veering off in the wrong direction. "I'm not saying the guy's actually breaking into rooms. Even a shady lawyer would be way too smart for that. No, I'm thinking it's probably more like he's in collusion with the burglar. Maybe Ross carries the stolen property back to the States to sell. Who knows? He could be running a whole network of resort burglars."

Lana had to suck her lips between her teeth to keep from smiling. Even with the resort holding an axe over her head, she couldn't help seeing the ridiculousness of Mark's scenario. For some time, she had known that Mark was smitten with Carrie. What hadn't been clear until now was just how deeply jealous he was of Ben Ross.

"Okay, that's my guess," he said. "Let's hear yours."

She shook her head. "As I said, I don't have a clue."

Lana managed to steer Mark onto other, less troublesome topics. But as he rattled on about the rising price of airline fares, Lana glanced back at the swimming pool.

Her gaze lingered on Arnold and Sybil Rodgers as she recalled all the times they had remained behind at the resort, one or both of them missing scheduled side excursions because of a seemingly endless series of ailments and unlucky mishaps. And the couple did haul a lot of luggage back from their island trips.

Chapter Ten

Sunset filled the room with a pinkish glow. Carrie checked the bedside clock as she put the last pins in her hair, which she had swept up off her neck in an elaborate twist. Ben was due at her door in less than ten minutes.

A flutter of anticipation seized her stomach.

She felt guilty about traipsing off to the dinner party while Galaxy Tours was in crisis and her job was hanging by a thread. But Lana had insisted, pointing out that this would very likely be her one and only chance to rub elbows with *the* Sam Rivers.

True, spending an evening with the world famous stage and film actor was a giant step beyond Carrie's wildest fantasy. But now that the moment had almost arrived, she realized that the prospect of being in Ben's company once again was what really filled her with excitement.

It was a bittersweet excitement at that. Ben would be returning to Boston soon. In all likelihood, this would be the last evening they would spend together.

That thought stole the light from her eyes.

Carrie stared blindly into the mirror over the dresser as she awakened to an even deeper realization. Somehow, somewhere, at some time over the past few days, she had begun to fall for Ben Ross. She didn't understand how her feelings for Price Carmichael's emissary could have taken such a turn. But there it was, buried like a ripening seed in her heart.

A knock sounded on the door.

Startled, Carrie checked her watch. Ben was six minutes early—for some reason, she had expected him to arrive right on the dot. Her stomach gave another flutter that felt perilously close to stage fright. Hopping along first on one foot, then the other as she slipped into her heels, she hurried to open the door.

"Oh . . . hello, Mark."

Mark Hanes blinked, his gaze sweeping up and down her new dress. He was all spruced up in a pastel sports coat that flattered his tan. He must have made a pass through the resort's salon that afternoon, because his hair had gone from orange to platinum-blond. Carrie pretended not to notice, a task made easier when Mark held out a small bouquet of flowers.

"I know this is kind of late to be asking you to dinner, Carrie, but—"

"This is really sweet of you, Mark." Accepting the bouquet, she buried her nose in the blossoms, genuinely touched. No one had ever given her flowers before. But Ben gave you butterflies, she reminded herself.

Mark smiled. "I thought maybe the Sand Dollar would—"

"I'm sorry, but I'm afraid I was just getting ready to go out." After a pause, Carrie added, "With someone."

His smile died away. He didn't say anything. He just stood there, red-faced, stretching the awkward moment on and on.

Mark was the last person Carrie had expected to find at her door. It took her a moment to get her mind back into tour guide mode and come up with a solution.

"But I would love to have breakfast with you." She smiled and made a point of sniffing the flowers again. "Will you be free in the morning?"

"Well . . . sure." Mark jammed his hands deep into his pockets. "That would be great."

He shuffled his feet. They exchanged a few more pleasantries before he finally wished her a good evening and moved off down the hallway. Carrie watched him go. She didn't want to seem rude by closing the door too quickly. When he reached the corner, he glanced back. She gave him a little wave.

As soon as Mark was out of sight, Carrie dashed into

her room and grabbed an ice bucket. She added a few inches of water from the bathroom tap, and was just settling the bouquet into its emergency vase when another knock sounded on her door.

She checked the time again. Right on the button. As expected, her date was as punctual as a precision chronometer.

This time when she opened the door, she found Ben pacing back and forth in the hallway. He stopped and executed a crisp about-face. Carrie watched the pupils in his eyes dilate. Two beats later, he broke into a wide grin that brought a warm flush to her cheeks.

"Wow," he said simply.

"Thanks." She smiled. "Wow back at ya."

His wore his white dinner jacket as casually as if it were a favorite old sweatshirt. Of course, Carrie thought, he was accustomed to moving in circles where hand-tailored dinner jackets were commonplace. *Imagine that.* She was glad now that she had taken Lana's advice and splurged on the outfit.

Ben cocked one elbow with an excess of gallantry. "Let's go wow Sam and Trish."

Carrie snatched up her evening bag, locked the door to her room and slipped her arm through his. As they headed down the hallway, she was struck by how right it felt be with Ben.

Ben had rented a car for the evening. They drove east along the coastal highway in the direction of Falmouth, the soft tropical evening pouring in through the open windows. Carrie had never quite gotten used to traveling along on the left side of the road, but Ben seemed at ease with the Jamaican rules, so she relaxed, feeling safe. And when he reached over and took her hand, she felt even better than safe.

The feeling lasted all the way to their turn south near Half Moon Bay, and then down the narrow cutback road past Orange Valley in the deepening twilight.

"I get the feeling you're driving along on auto-pilot," Carrie said.

"Yeah, I've been this way a dozen or so times. Sam has had this place since he made his second movie sixteen years ago."

"You've known him that long?"

"Longer. We were roomies at Harvard."

Carrie sat up straighter. "You knew Sam Rivers when he was nobody?"

Ben laughed softly. "Sam was never a nobody, Carrie. Not even when he graduated in the bottom ten percent of our class. He's always been—special."

She eyed him for a moment. "You sound a little envious."

"I'm green with it."

"Because Sam is famous?" It couldn't be the money, Carrie thought. Ben obviously wasn't hurting in that department.

"Oh, it definitely isn't the fame." He glanced at her, then returned his attention to the road. His smile faded.

Just when Carrie had decided he was going to leave it at that, he added, "I envy Sam because he has exactly what he wants in life." He fell silent for another moment. "And he knows how to enjoy it."

"Don't you have what you want in life?"

Another pause. "I thought I did."

Carrie puzzled over his wistful tone. The more she got to know Ben, the less he seemed to fit the mold she had put him in.

Every now and then, they passed couples—even entire families—ambling along the side of the road, enjoying the after-sunset cool-down. Occasional snatches of music from unseen radios wafted on the evening air, weaving their sounds into dreamlike textures of the evening.

"What about you?" Ben asked. "Where do you want to be, say, ten years from now?"

Carrie gave a dry laugh. "Besides hoping to have made a major dent in paying back my student loans?"

She had been concentrating so hard on the day-to-day struggle of working herself through college that she hadn't really thought about what lay ahead after she graduated—when she finally crossed that giant hurdle. She gave it five full minutes of thought now.

"Oh," she said at last, "I guess ten years from now, I don't want to look back and be disappointed in myself."

Ben flicked a glance at her. "What would disappoint you?"

That took several additional moments, because it

was more of a feeling than a thought. She had trouble putting words to it.

"Not having made a difference," she said, wondering why Ben was asking these probing questions.

Carrie was about to risk putting a blemish on the evening by asking him if he was asking for himself, or as Price Carmichael's attorney, when he slowed and made a sharp right into an unmarked driveway. The hardtop surface snaked through stands of overhanging trees. In the distance, lights shone through dense foliage near the crest of a hill.

"I didn't expect his house to be so far off the beaten track," she said.

"The price of fame. Don't get me wrong—Sam loves and appreciates his fans. But there's a limit. Years back, he was having lunch at Johnny Cash's place over near Rose Hall, and spotted tourists spying on them from the bushes. He couldn't hack that. When he's not out promoting a film, Sam and Trish value their privacy."

Near the top of the hill, the driveway widened onto a paved parking area already packed with cars—everything from a sedate white Volvo station wagon to a flashy red Mercedes sports car. Carrie thought of her rusty old clunker back in Atlanta, and already felt way out of her league.

Ben parked, and they got out. Taking her hand, he led her through an old-fashioned wooden-picket gate set into a fragrant hedge. The gate opened onto a flagstone courtyard fronting a sprawling low-roofed house, its large windows shielded by louvered plantation shutters. Beyond a splashing triple-tier fountain off to the left, hooded lights shone through the trees.

"That's the tennis court," Ben said, catching her peering at the lights. "Don't ever let Sam talk you into playing. He'll bait you with a few easy lobs, then run you straight into the ground."

Fat chance of her ever walking onto a court with *the* Sam Rivers, Carrie thought. Besides, the closest she had ever come to playing tennis was a game of Ping-pong.

At the door, Ben pressed the doorbell, then opened the door without waiting. The muted six-note chime reminded Carrie of the theme music to her favorite Sam Rivers movie. The tune was still sounding as they stepped into a spacious foyer off which three hallways radiated.

For just a few seconds, they stood there, hand-in-hand, listening to a murmur of voices punctuated by bursts of laughter coming from somewhere deep in the house. Carrie chewed her lip in anticipation of wading in way over her head.

A door closed nearby, followed by the sound of footsteps lightly running over polished marble. A woman's voice called, "Benjie?"

Ben winced as Carrie arched a brow at him. He shook his head, and called back, "It's us, Trish."

Carrie glimpsed a froth of white and turned toward the center hallway as a tiny red-haired woman in a simple gown flew into Ben's arms. The woman squealed like a schoolgirl as he swung her around twice before setting her down.

"Trish, when are you going to ditch that slob and run away with me?" Ben asked, pecking her on the cheek.

She laughed and turned to Carrie. "I'm Trish," she said, taking both of Carrie's hands. "Sam's better half. You must be the incredible Caroline we've heard so much about this week."

Carrie shot a look at Ben. He was busy examining the high ceiling as if he had never noticed it before.

"It was nice of you to invite me, Trish," Carrie said.

"Oh, it was our pleasure entirely. Sam and I have been dying of curiosity ever since Ben phoned." Trish winked, lowering her voice. "You're the first woman he's ever brought home."

"Home?"

"That's us." Trish glanced over her shoulder at Ben without letting go of Carrie's hands. "Benjie seemed to need a home base, so I sort of adopted him when Sam and I got married. I have a soft spot for stray mutts."

Carrie watched Trish exchange a look of warm, easy affection with Ben, and found that she liked the woman a lot. Her gaze drifted past Trish to the arched doorway to the central hall. She blinked as a flash of recognition hit her.

Sam Rivers stood in the doorway with his hands clasped behind his back, smiling at them. The first thing that struck Carrie was that he wasn't nearly as tall as he appeared on the big screen. Then other details rushed at her.

Like Ben, he wore a white dinner jacket. But he had at least a two-day growth of beard stubble, and possibly the worst haircut she had ever seen. She tried to come up with a one word description of his appearance, and settled on *dissipated*. In spite of that, she was mesmerized by his celebrated quicksilver-gray eyes—the very ones that transfixed audiences the world over with an incredible range of emotion, from tearful grief to unrequited love to towering rage.

At the moment, they held only amused curiosity.

She stopped breathing as he took her in from head to toe.

"Caroline," he said, finally.

Her name rolled off his tongue. The sound of warm molasses, she thought. With a broad grin, *the* Sam Rivers crossed the foyer and enveloped Carrie in a welcoming embrace. She stood wide-eyed in his arms, his beard stubble scratching her cheek, aware that with her three-inch heels they were virtually the same height.

"Don't overdo it, Sam," Ben said after awhile.

"Get away, sleaze bag." Sam made no move to release her. "You don't deserve this treasure."

"I'm sure Carrie agrees."

Sam stepped back at last and cuffed Ben on the shoulder. "Good to see you, *compadre*. How've you been since the old man died?"

Ben flicked his gaze at Carrie and wiped a hand

across his mouth. Sam picked up on the body language at once, and grimaced.

"That's right . . . my apologies." He touched Carrie's arm. "Please accept my condolences, Caroline. I forgot that Price Carmichael was your uncle."

"You also forgot to shave," Ben said, wrenching the conversation onto a different track. "I thought you'd finished that derelict-cowboy flick."

Sam scratched his bristly jaw. "Two more days of reshooting at the end of the month."

His shoulders slumped. He gave Caroline a hangdog look. Suddenly, magically, it was as if he was standing there in front of her in rundown boots, with a battered Stetson clutched in both hands.

"Miss Caroline," he drawled, "I'd be purely beholden to you if you'd see fit to let me rustle you up a glass of spring water with a twist of lime."

Carrie's tension fled. She was starstruck, no doubt about it. Even so, she could not get over how ordinary all this felt. She sensed that beneath all the glitz and glamour, Sam and Trish Rivers were just nice, regular people.

"By the way, you're needed out on the terrace, Ben," Trish said, hooking an arm through his and aiming him toward the hallway on the left. "Old Dexter Wilde has come up with a scheme that requires your legal expertise."

Ben glanced back at Carrie and gave her a helpless shrug as Sam maneuvered her in the opposite direction.

Dexter Wilde, she thought, dazzled. Just last year,

the movie director had received a lifetime achievement Oscar. And he needed advice from Ben. . . .

Sam ushered her into a vast sunken great room filled with deeply cushioned rattan furniture. A pair of lighted ceiling fans turned slowly. Across the room, an entire wall of French doors stood open to the tropical night. Outside, what appeared to be a couple of dozen guests in dinner jackets and evening dresses milled around on a sweeping flagstone terrace. Beyond them, lights glowed softly at the bottom of a big kidney-shaped swimming pool.

From the living room, Carrie watched Trish lead Ben through the guests toward a rotund man with a gray walrus mustache who was seated in a wingback wicker chair near the pool's diving board. Dexter Wilde in the flesh. Carrie had a disorienting sense that she had stepped onto a Hollywood movie set.

"Was our divide-and-conquer routine convincing?" Sam asked, moving over to a long table filled with ice buckets, crystal glasses, and several trays of canapés. "Or did Trish and I overact?"

Carrie looked at him. "Pardon?"

He laughed. "Please don't be offended by my prying, Caroline. I'm just curious. Ben's like a brother, and he obviously thinks you're special or he wouldn't have brought you home. So I wanted a few minutes alone with you so we could get acquainted. Trish and I mean no harm."

Home. That was the second time Carrie had heard

Calypso Wind

the Rivers household labeled as Ben's home. That made her wonder.

"Ben mentioned that you had built on a room for him," she said, "but I didn't realize you were so close. He hasn't said much about his real family."

"My guess is that he's said absolutely nothing about them."

Sam opened a bottle of spring water, poured it over chipped ice in a stemmed glass, and added a twist of lime. He handed Carrie the glass, leaned back against the table, and folded his arms.

Carrie rattled the ice in the glass. Lips pursed in thought, she gazed out toward where Ben had pulled up a chair next to Dexter Wilde. The two men were engaged in what appeared to be an intense conversation. Judging from the way they sat with their elbows on their knees, practically head to head, she got the impression that this wasn't the first time they had met.

"What are they like?" she asked Sam. "Ben's real family."

The actor reached back and plucked a cracker topped with cheese and celery from the tray. He popped it into his mouth, watching her carefully as he chewed, taking his time before answering.

"Well, he doesn't have a *real* family, Caroline. He grew up in foster homes."

Carrie rocked back. "You're serious?"

"As rain. When he was a senior in high school, he got a part-time job as assistant to the groundskeeper on

Price Carmichael's estate. Backbreaking work, because the head groundskeeper dumped all the coolie labor on him. But he stuck it out. You see, he had a dream of going to college, and knew nobody was going to hand him that on a silver platter."

She stared at Sam. "I, uhm, can identify with that."

"Well, after a few months, Ben discovered that the groundskeeper was padding expenses and pocketing the excess. As much as he needed the job, he couldn't stomach dishonesty, so Ben warned the guy to knock it off. When that didn't do any good, Ben reported it to your uncle even though he figured the old man would be so furious that he would fire both of them. But Carmichael must have seen something in Ben. Instead of firing him, he took Ben under his wing. The rest, as they say, is history."

Carrie was speechless.

"Mind you," Sam continued, helping himself to another cracker, "it took me years to wheedle all this out of Ben in little dribs and drabs. I'm telling it to you now in case you've been wondering why he's so intensely loyal to your uncle. He sees Carmichael as a father figure—the father he never had. And in truth, he owes Carmichael a lot."

"Owes? My uncle put him through college?"

Sam nodded. "He paid Carmichael back every cent though—with interest. That's the kind of guy Ben is. When we met as Harvard freshmen, both of us were financial hardship cases. Lived like a couple of monks,

Calypso Wind

we did." He grinned wryly for several seconds, remembering, then looked her in the eye. "But Ben didn't accept one thin dime more than he had to from his mentor."

Carrie was grateful to Sam for explaining so much. Now that the initial shock of being around him was wearing off, how she felt about being around the film star had undergone an unexpected change. Instead of being awestruck just being in his presence, she sensed a comforting camaraderie developing between them.

So much so that she returned his gaze evenly. "Did you get to know my uncle, Sam?"

He hesitated, as if carefully choosing his words. "Ben hasn't talked much about your relationship with your uncle, Caroline. He's discreet about his business dealings. But as I've said, he and I are close." He waved a hand, as if gathering an invisible object from the air. "And I've picked up a vague impression that you might have . . . issues with Carmichael."

She nodded once, deeply.

"Then let me say that I'm aware that Carmichael had his detractors," Sam said, apparently feeling he was on safer ground.

"You're being very tactful," she said.

His smile came and went. "So let me guess—you're wondering how much of Price Carmichael rubbed off on Ben."

Carrie hadn't thought about it in those terms—not precisely—but she had to admit that Sam was on target.

Sam pushed away from the table. Picking up the bottle of spring water, he came over and refilled her glass.

"Caroline, you need to know something, assuming that you haven't figured it out already. There's a basic decency in Ben that goes clear to the bone. It's a quality that runs far too deep to become tainted by outside influences." He tilted a crooked smile, leaving her uncle's name out of it. "Have you noticed how animals are drawn to him?"

"And babies." *And me.*

He chuckled. "Funny thing is, he doesn't seem to realize that's unusual."

Carrie sighed. At last she knew now why it was so important to Ben that she sign the inheritance contract and return to Boston. The contract would guarantee continuity of the Carmichael name and legacy that he valued so dearly.

She sighed again, wishing for his sake that she could go along with the plan. But Ben's dream was her own worst nightmare.

Ben knew the exact moment when Carrie stepped out of the great room, where Sam had kept her corralled for the past twenty-seven minutes. Though his back was to the French doors, he sensed her presence on the terrace, as if the very air around him had taken on a different feel.

He turned in his chair and watched Trish lead Carrie from one cluster of guests to the next, making intro-

Calypso Wind 157

ductions. At first, Carrie looked a little dazed. But after awhile, she put on a smile as big as the sun and began mingling. With a smile of his own, Ben realized that in desperation, she was falling back on her tour guide training.

She seemed to have stumbled onto something that he hadn't really recognized until now, Ben thought. Just about everything in life was play-acting, in one form or another. Even the society mavens back on Beacon Hill in Boston played roles on a stage reserved exclusively for themselves.

He continued to watch, conscious that Carrie possessed a kind of inner dignity and poise that seemed to make her skin glow. Just watching her move from group to group, her dress shimmering in the dancing light from tiki torches, made his chest feel tight. He already knew that, on down the road, this was an image that he would take out and examine again and again.

"Is that the lady in question?" asked Dexter Wilde.

Ben straightened and cleared his throat. Once Carrie stepped out onto the terrace, he had completely lost track of his conversation with the director.

"Yes, Dexter," he said. "That's her in the blue dress."

Wilde leaned back in his chair and studied Carrie from afar.

"Well," he said, "your Miss Washburn does have a certain stage presence. Can she act?"

After giving the question some thought, Ben decided to leave it unanswered.

He had a sense that Carrie could do just about anything she put her mind to, including acting. But beyond erecting a cheerful tour guide façade in order to conceal her nervousness, he doubted that she would find much appeal in pretending to be someone she wasn't.

Excusing himself, Ben hoisted himself to his feet and moved across the terrace as casually as he could manage. He hung back for a moment as Trish introduced Carrie to yet another cluster of guests. Then he stepped in and slid an arm around Carrie's slender waist.

"Come with me," he whispered.

She looked startled, then pleased. "Where to?"

"I want to show you the tennis court."

As Ben walked Carrie down a series of deep flagstone steps leading off the east end of the terrace, Trish's amused gaze burned into his back. But the sheer pleasure of being with Carrie was worth any price.

"Careful," he said. "Since the hurricane last fall, the path is a little uneven in places."

"We could use a flashlight." Carrie leaned closer against him as they moved along the winding path. "It's dark as a closet under these trees."

"Yeah, it is. We seem to be in the grips of a sudden electrical outage." The lights tucked into the landscaping had blinked off the moment they stepped off the terrace. "I should have warned you—Sam thinks he has an eye for set decoration."

"Are you saying this entire evening is a staged production?"

He groaned. "That was not my intention, Carrie. But Sam and Trish tend to overstep their bounds where I'm concerned."

"They obviously care a lot for you."

"They meddle."

She smiled, gazing up at the stars as they walked. "That's what friends are for."

Without thinking, Ben said, "And you, Carrie? Are you a friend?"

After a lengthy pause, she said, "I hope so."

He let out a slow breath so she wouldn't noticed, surprised by the flood of relief precipitated by those three words. She couldn't know how much of a gift she had just handed him. Carrie Washburn had a mind of her own, especially where her uncle was concerned, and Ben simply hadn't expected her to allow herself to be friends with Price Carmichael's lawyer.

The pathway curved sharply to the left. Ben took Carrie's hand and led her onto a small secluded terrace where water from a mermaid fountain splashed in the moonlight. The scented night breeze riffled the hem of her dress and wafted invisible fingers through loose tendrils of hair floating at her neck. He touched her hair himself, fingering a silky wisp of honey.

"I like that smile," he said. "What's behind it?"

"I was just thinking. Of all the tropical islands I've

been to as a tour guide, this is the first time I've really, truly realized how romantic they can be."

Ben suddenly felt dumbstruck. She was probably expecting him to say something appropriate—definitely something romantic—but the words wouldn't surface. Not for the first time while he was near Carrie, he felt like a rank adolescent, green and unsure of himself. All he could do was gaze at her with a sense of pure wonder.

After a moment, she said, "I, uhm, thought you were going to show me the tennis court." She sounded as strained as he felt.

"Right. It's over there." Without taking his gaze off her, Ben indicated a glow of lights some distance away, screened in by a tall vine-draped lattice fence.

The proper words remained locked up in some hidden closet inside him, but he wasn't out and out paralyzed. Not even close. Ben turned his back to the lights, blocking them from Carrie's view. She looked up at him, her face like the shadow of a dream in the pale moonlight as he slid his arms around her.

She didn't resist, but he felt cautious tension in her body. Ben gently cupped the back of her head with one hand, his thumb curling around to feel the quickening pulse on the side of her throat.

"You look incredible tonight, Carrie," he said.

Her throat spasmed, making a faint clicking sound as she swallowed. "You look pretty irresistible yourself . . . Benjie."

Calypso Wind

He growled again, smiling. "Please, don't call me that. Makes me sound like a shaggy mutt."

She laughed softly and spread both hands across his chest, thumb to thumb, as if measuring its breadth. With a deep sigh, he bent and brushed his lips across her moonlit cheeks, right then left.

"Sweet Carrie," he murmured, pulling her close, finding her lips as her arms slid around his neck.

Friends. Even as the word drifted through his mind on satin wings, some part of him knew they were becoming much more than that. The prospect both excited and terrified him.

Ben was vaguely aware of something nudging insistently against his left ankle, accompanied by a rumbling sound like a distant outboard motor. He ignored it until Carrie gave a little gasp and broke their kiss.

She had a dreamy look in her eyes that he thought might have been just a trick of the moonlight. He felt pretty dreamy himself at the moment. When he started to lean into another kiss, she took his hand and pressed his palm to her warm lips.

"What's so funny?" he asked hoarsely, feeling her smile.

"Haven't you noticed?" A playful grin in her voice.

Ben took half a step back and stumbled over something. The obstacle darted off a few feet, a shadow among shadows. He was still trying to figure out what it was when it quickly returned to purr tight figure eights against his leg.

"Trish's cat," he muttered. "She probably sent it to spy on us."

Carrie laughed outright. Ben wondered what she found so funny about an aging, overweight cat.

She picked up the big ginger feline and scratched it under the chin. The purring grew louder, breaking into rattling, choking sounds as the cat attempted to squirm onto its back in her arms.

"Well, then," she said. "Maybe you'd better show me the tennis court in case Trish springs a snap quiz on us."

Ben kept an arm around Carrie's shoulders as they strolled along a series of interconnecting pathways, the big cat sounding like a local tour bus rumbling along in her arms. The feel of Ben's lips lingered on hers, warm as the sun. She let her eyes drift shut, breathing in the scented night air, trusting Ben not to lead her astray. Trusting Ben.

"That cat sheds like a son of a gun," he said.

She nuzzled against its ginger coat. "Nobody's perfect."

After a long moment of silence, Ben said, "Hold that thought."

Carrie's eyes popped open. She stopped and looked up at Ben. His thumb stroked her cheek, as gentle as the night breeze. He hadn't been talking about the cat, she thought. He had meant for her to hold that thought about him—the part about nobody being perfect.

"Ben, I'm not sure what you—"

He pressed a finger lightly across her lips and made a shushing sound. His lips touched her forehead with the weight of a whisper. Then he tucked her back under his arm and they walked on—a man, a woman, and a contented cat.

In the snug quiet that had built between them, Carrie realized that she was no longer just attracted to Ben Ross. She was falling hopelessly, helplessly in love with him.

Chapter Eleven

Dark, colorless rain lashed the closed French doors in the great room, obliterating the view of the flagstone terrace outside. All the tiki torches had gone out. The swimming pool lights cast only a faint glow through the continuing deluge.

The sudden storm had run its course as a topic of conversation during dinner, and now was being roundly ignored by the guests crowded into the sunken room.

Caught up in the stimulating table chatter around her, Carrie had barely touched the delicious pineapple-chicken and rice pilaf, with feather-light yeast rolls that Trish had baked herself. Dessert had been a frothy tropical-fruit and ice-cream confection served in small, individual terra cotta flowerpots. After Sam practically inhaled his dessert, Carrie had jokingly offered him

Calypso Wind 165

hers. He had accepted with a childlike crow of delight, roundly ignoring Trish's chiding that Dexter would have to shoot Sam with a wide-angle lens if he didn't rope in his sweet tooth.

Now Carrie sat alone on a rattan settee somewhat removed from the thick of the gathered guests, feeling hungrier than she should be after such a spread.

Off and on, she peered at her reflection in the door glass. She had to employ every atom of her willpower not to keep glancing across the room to where Ben had been cornered by a trio of gray-haired banker types. If she stared at him long enough, he invariably looked up and met her gaze, as if responding to some palpable signal. When he did, his eyes fairly cried out with impatience.

She smiled to herself, enjoying an odd sensation that she was radiating light. She could maintain that imagined glow, she found, just as long as she didn't allow herself to think of Price Carmichael.

A hand touched her shoulder from behind.

Carrie looked up to find Sam Rivers grinning languidly at her. She was growing accustomed to the scruffy beard stubble, the butchered hair, and the surprisingly short stature. His famous matinee-idol eyes could still make her feel like a giddy fan, but she realized they didn't stir her as Ben's eyes could.

"Hey, gorgeous," he said, moving around in front of her. "Don't tell me that sleazy lawyer has abandoned you."

Carrie shot a glance across the room. One of the banker types had a hand firmly clamped on Ben's arm. "Actually, Ben appears to have been taken hostage by a pack of stuffy Wall Street paper shufflers."

"Ah, a fate worse than death." He leaned in closer to stage-whisper, "They're deep pockets, looking to bankroll a movie I want to do. I think they're trying to get Ben to convince them that they'll clean up at the box office."

"Would Ben know that?"

"*Nobody* knows how a film will do, Caroline. That's what's so exhilarating about this business. But suits trust suits—that's in their genetic makeup. Investors would rather talk out their insecurities with a fellow pin-striper than with a Hollywood producer."

Sam shifted his weight, and Carrie noticed the rotund man standing behind him—the only person in the room to whom she hadn't been formally introduced that evening. More than once, she had wondered if that omission had been by design. She had caught him watching her from time to time, eyes narrowed, as if he were judging the good or bad attributes of a racehorse. Perhaps because of that, she had found him intimidating even from afar.

"Carrie, it's time you got together with Dexter Wilde here." Sam stepped aside and motioned to the older man. "Dexter will direct *and* produce my next film, and just incidentally he's richer than Donald Trump. As you've probably noticed, he's been picking Ben's brain

Calypso Wind

this evening. Now he wants to bend your lovely, shell-like ear."

Dexter laughed easily. He offered Carrie a pudgy hand sporting a pinky ring with a grape-sized ruby. Carrie shook hands, dry-mouthed at being the focus of the legendary director's attention.

"May I join you?" he asked, indicating the settee.

"Of course."

Carrie tried to relax as he settled his formidable bulk onto the deep floral-print cushion. Close up, Dexter Wilde didn't seem at all overbearing. Instead, he had warm, intelligent eyes that measured her without seeming to be calculating. Her self-confidence perked up.

"Directing films must be exciting," she said, thinking of Brad Pitt, Julia Roberts, and a host of others who had starred in Dexter-directed movies.

"Oh, yes." Wilde smiled. "So is producing—knowing how easily you can lose your shirt."

"Don't take him seriously, Carrie." Sam gave the director a courtly bow. "Dexter has lots of shirts."

Trish slipped up next to Sam, tucked her arm through his, and looked expectantly at each of them in turn. "Well?" She raised her brows at Wilde. "What did Carrie say?"

The director chuckled. "Slow down, my dear. I haven't had a chance to pop the question."

"Oops." Trish pressed her fingertips to her lips.

"Oops, indeed." Sam bared his teeth at Trish. With a

jaunty three-fingered salute to Carrie, he turned and led his wife away.

Carrie frowned slightly, watching them go. She sensed a puzzling undercurrent of intrigue.

Wilde stretched a thick arm across the back of the settee and leaned closer, his expression going somber. "Ben has told me quite a lot about you, Miss Washburn."

"Oh?" The abrupt change in his demeanor startled her. She glanced after Sam and Trish. They had joined a couple over by the rain-swept French doors. Across the room, Ben still hadn't managed to extricate himself from his captors.

Up close, Wilde was eyeing her as he had all evening, measuring her in some way. Carrie had seen that a lot lately, first from Ben, then from Sam and Trish Rivers. But this was the first time she had felt as though she were auditioning for something. She didn't have the slightest clue why, and had even less of an idea what that something might be.

"But I seem to have you at a disadvantage," Wilde said. "So now let me tell you a little about myself."

"I already know quite a lot about you, Mr. Wilde," she said. "I watched the Oscars ceremony—that was a beautiful tribute to your career."

He waved a hand in a gesture of dismissal. "A fluff piece, dealing only with my successes," he said. "The real story goes back forty years, to when I made my first film on a shoestring. It flopped miserably. But I didn't let go of the dream. I scratched around for more financing and made a second film, then a third, each one of them a box-office bomb."

He smiled, as if looking back on the string of early failures with a certain fondness. "That's the part of my career that you don't hear about at awards ceremonies, Miss Washburn."

"I didn't know."

"Those years matter to no one but me." He tapped himself on the chest. "The important thing is that, eventually, I gained enough experience to succeed."

"Spectacularly!" Carrie wondered why he was telling her all this.

"Yes, my dear. I have been blessed." He dipped his head in what appeared to be genuine humility. "But even after more than a dozen profitable films, I've never forgotten the earliest lesson—that success rarely comes easily."

She nodded, reminded of her long, continuing struggle to get through college. Success on a scale of Dexter Wilde's wasn't even on her wildest pie-in-the-sky wish list, but she understood the labor involved in making a dream come true.

"Miss Washburn," he continued, "as Sam so baldly indicated, I've made myself fairly rich over the years. Now I'm getting on in years, and I feel it's time for me to give back to society some of what it has so generously given to me."

"That's wonderful," Carrie said.

"On the contrary—I see it as a duty. Therefore, I'm in the process of creating a non-profit foundation to help young people who are willing to work their hearts out to make their dreams come true, just like I did."

"Really?" Carrie sat up straighter, wondering if she should mention Winston Brown and Gordon Darnell.

"Really. These days, as you know, education is everything. Without higher learning, the seeds of most dreams haven't a chance of germinating."

Carrie nodded. Evidently, the director's foundation had to do with college scholarships. Her hopes for Winston and Gordon sagged. But she still didn't understand what Dexter Wilde was getting at, or why he kept looking at her with such intensity. Was it possible that he was working his way around to offering her funding for her college tuition?

But why me?

"How am I doing so far, Miss Washburn?" he asked.

"Your foundation sounds very . . . interesting." That seemed like an understatement, but she didn't know what else to say.

"I'm delighted that you approve." He patted his hand on the back of the settee, as if indicating a new phase in the conversation. "You see, Miss Washburn, I'm searching for a special person who can screen young applicants, and present suitable candidates to my foundation's board."

"Oh." Before disappointment for her own sake had a

Calypso Wind 171

chance to set in, Carrie remembered Lester Darnell's big dream of going to college.

The boy was way too young for that now. But he was bright and hard-working, and as Carrie's mother used to say, tomorrow was just around the corner.

"Ben assures me that you are an excellent judge of character," Wilde said.

Startled from a vision of Lester Darnell marching across a stage in a cap and gown, Carrie stared at Wilde. "Ben said that?"

He gave a deep nod. "What's more, Ben is quite insistent that you have a natural empathy for industrious people in need of a helping hand." He smiled, pausing for a moment to study her again. "In fact, unless I'm badly mistaken, you're thinking of a likely candidate right this second."

"I am?"

"Quickly—a name."

"Lester Darnell."

He smiled. "See?"

"Lester is just a boy now, but he—"

Wilde held up a hand like a traffic cop. "There will be time for that, Miss Washburn."

Carrie glanced across the room at Ben and caught him watching her. She had a peculiar feeling that Wilde had already heard Lester's name before—maybe straight from Ben's mouth. She still didn't know where she was supposed to fit into this picture.

"The individual who screens applicants for my foundation," Wilde said, "will shoulder a heavy responsibility. That's why we're looking for someone who will feel committed to the job."

"I can just imagine."

Whoever the screener turned out to be, Carrie wanted the name. Sometime in the future, she would be sending along Lester Darnell's application.

"I believe you might be the right person, my dear." Wilde pointed a stubby finger at her. "Will you consider accepting the job?"

Flabbergasted. That's how Carrie felt—head-over-heels flabbergasted. Her mouth hung open. She couldn't seem to make it shut.

Wilde looked amused. "Forgive me if I shocked you. Perhaps I should have asked Ben to soften you up first, before I dropped this onto your lap."

"Soften me up?"

He chuckled. "You're still in school yourself, I understand. Working with my foundation would be quite a feather in your resume. But taking on substantial volunteer responsibilities before you graduate is bound to put you under a good deal of pressure."

Volunteer? "There wouldn't be a salary?"

He looked surprised. "Well, no, there wouldn't. As I've already mentioned, the foundation will be a non-profit, Miss Washburn. We don't want to go spending money on needless administrative overhead, do we?"

Calypso Wind 173

"But . . ." Carrie gave an embarrassed laugh, the heat of a florid blush rising up her neck. "How would I eat?"

Wilde frowned. "Eat?" Then he, too, fired a glance across the room toward Ben. "I assumed . . ."

Carrie waited for him to continue. When he didn't, slow awareness began to seep in, transforming the hollow of her stomach into a fiery cauldron even as her fisted hands turned to ice.

"Oh, I see." She raised her chin, forcing herself to look Wilde in the eye. "You must have heard a rumor that I was about to move to Boston." *And that I was about to become independently wealthy—so I could afford to volunteer for a fulltime non-paying job.*

The director met her gaze. She saw in his baffled expression that she had guessed correctly.

"I'm Price Carmichael's niece, Mr. Wilde," she said. "I assure you, that's as far as my connection with him goes. If you really want to know, I'm one of those hard-working dreamers you talked about, in the flesh. I'm working my way through college, trying to make my own dream come true. So I'm afraid I won't be able to accept a non-paying job. But I'm flattered by the offer."

The director's hand tap-tap-tapped on the back of the settee as he ruminated. He frowned at his lap for quite a long time, then grunted. "Hmm."

"Mr. Wilde, I'm sorry if I—"

He held up a hand again—a man accustomed to giving stage directions. "No, no, my dear. You have nothing to be sorry for. I'm the one who should be apologizing. There seems to have been a misunderstanding. Perhaps I misjudged . . ."

Carrie realized that Dexter Wilde was every bit as embarrassed as she was. She scrabbled in vain for something to say that might smooth over the awkwardness.

After a moment, Wilde gathered himself together and heaved his substantial bulk off the settee. He stood there looking down at her, frowning slightly as if in deep thought. "Do forgive me if I've been presumptuous, Miss Washburn. Perhaps we'll talk again in the future."

She managed a smile that hurt at the corners. "Perhaps."

The smile melted as she watched the director walk away.

The settee suddenly felt like a desolate island. Carrie tried to shrug off the encounter, but she couldn't get over the sense that she had somehow failed Lester.

Chapter Twelve

Before the cushion that Dexter Wilde had occupied had a chance to cool, Trish Rivers swooped in to take his place. Her frothy evening gown settled in around her like a white cloud. Carrie wanted to be upset with her, but found that she couldn't. From the get-go, Trish had seemed too much like the sister that Carrie had never had.

"How did that go?" Trish asked.

"Let's just say it was one of the most humiliating moments in my life." That was as close as she could come to it without being rude.

Trish appeared to deflate. "Carrie, we didn't mean to—"

"Be honest with me, Trish," Carrie interrupted, as humiliation metamorphosed into a different animal altogether. "Did Ben engineer that set-up? Or was he just acting on something that you and Sam had arranged?"

"You mean about Dexter's foundation?" Trish looked sheepish, then her lips parted on a throaty laugh. "No, Carrie, it wasn't like that at all. Dexter told Sam about his idea before you and Ben arrived, and it just sort of snowballed. Please believe me."

Carrie did believe her. That helped to take the edge off the sting of humiliation. Just as Dexter Wilde had said, it had all been a misunderstanding. Nothing more.

"Besides," Trish said in an undertone, "unless I'm badly mistaken, Ben is way too lovesick to be thinking straight enough to set anyone up."

Lovesick?

For a moment, Trish disappeared into a milky haze. Through an eerie numbness, Carrie was vaguely aware of a cool hand gently stroking hers. Trish's melodious voice murmured words that she couldn't quite catch through the tinny roar in her ears.

Carrie's vision cleared just in time for her to watch Trish rise from the settee with the straight-backed grace of a dancer and drift off to mingle with her other guests.

Lovesick?

Across the room, Ben had finally extricated himself from the pin-striped suits and was working his way in her direction. Carrie monitored his progress with wildly mixed emotions.

He paused at the wingback chair where Dexter Wilde had resettled himself, and exchanged a few words with the aging director. Neither man so much as glanced toward Carrie, but Ben looked surprised by something Wilde said, and both men frowned as they parted.

Carrie stood and took a couple of deep breaths, preparing herself.

By the time Ben reached her, his expression was as unreadable as a plaster mask. His ability to hide his emotions like that was undoubtedly useful in a courtroom, but it left her feeling as if she were standing on quicksand.

On uncertain footing, she had a powerful urge to reach out to him for support as he stopped in front of her. But a warning sign kept flashing in the back of her mind—Ben Ross was first and foremost Price Carmichael's attorney—his substitute son. As such, he had a job to do. A job that entailed persuading Carrie, by whatever means necessary, to sign on the dotted line.

Maybe even using Dexter Wilde to tempt me into another world.

But that last didn't ring true. Not with Trish's words still reverberating through her, reinforcing her strange sense of vertigo.

Lovesick. Had Trish been joking?

Ben cocked his head and said, "Dexter seems troubled."

"It must be contagious."

He held her gaze forever, unblinking. A moment earlier, Carrie had been upset. But with Ben standing close enough to touch, a deeper emotion thrummed through her—one that gave her an unexpected sense of strength and conviction.

I have to know, she thought. That's all there is to it. This can't wait another minute.

Carrie glanced around. The evening was wearing down, and most of the other guests had settled into or around clustered seating arrangements. The settee was a bit off by itself, but not nearly far enough out of earshot for what she intended to ask.

She took Ben's arm and led him to a quiet corner over near the French doors. Rain lashing against the glass was plenty loud enough to cover their voices if they spoke quietly. She turned to face him.

"I want to know something, Ben. Right now, right here."

"I swear, Carrie, I did not sic Dexter onto you." He held up three fingers as if in a scout pledge, reminding her of Sam's perky little salute, and of the brotherhood the two men shared. "When we arrived this evening, Dexter hit me up about his foundation. It sounded like something that might interest you, so I aimed him in your direction. That's it."

"Fine. I believe you. But that isn't my question." Carrie glanced around again to make sure no one—namely Trish—was eavesdropping. Her throat had gone tight on her. She swallowed, trying to keep her courage scraped together.

"Dexter misunderstood about your financial circumstances," Ben continued as if he hadn't heard her. "And I, in turn, misunderstood his intentions. I had no idea he was looking for an unpaid volunteer."

"Are you in love with me?"

He froze, lips parted, both hands raised to accentuate his next point—a sincere attorney pleading his case before a jury. For a fleeting moment, he looked so vulnerable that Carrie's heart instantly went out to him, even as she knew that she had just made a terrible mistake.

Then the muscles in his jaw knotted and his eyes turned to steel.

He held out a hand. "Come with me."

Flushed with renewed embarrassment, she took a couple of seconds to reflect on how she had managed to single-handedly turn a fantasy evening into a total disaster. She shouldn't have come to a place where she didn't belong. She had gotten in over her head, and had no one to blame but herself.

She nevertheless balked at Ben's commanding tone. "I, uhm, want an answer first."

"Not here." He waggled his fingers, trying to hurry her along. "We can't do this here . . . you know that."

Carrie hesitated, wishing she could go back five minutes and pretend she had never let herself in for what was shaping up to be the humiliation of her life—of ten lifetimes—putting even her encounter with Dexter Wilde in the shade.

Lovesick, indeed. Of course, Trish had been joking, she saw that clearly now. Just because she was losing her heart to Ben didn't change reality, which was that he had come down to Jamaica with Price Carmichael on his mind and an inheritance contract in his pocket.

And rich tastes . . . don't forget that.

She glanced around at the other guests, who looked as at home in fancy dress as she felt in a T-shirt and old sweatpants.

The quicksand shifted. Off-balance, teetering in her mind, and physically aching all over, Carrie took his hand.

Gripping her hand just a little too tightly for comfort, Ben escorted her out of the great room and down a long hallway into a wing of the house that she hadn't seen before. At the end of the hallway, he pulled open a thick door lined with padded vinyl and swept a hand over a panel of light switches on the wall.

Soft, indirect lighting flooded the high ceiling of a large acoustic-paneled room. The red-carpeted floor sloped down in a succession of crescent-shaped tiers toward a wide projection screen on the opposite wall. Three rows of plush-upholstered chairs lined the tiers. To the right of the screen was another padded door, an emergency exit beneath a lit sign that read FLEE THIS WAY.

Ben marched Carrie down the center aisle of what

she realized was a miniature private movie theater, complete with stadium seating for about two dozen people. In the corner opposite the emergency exit stood a soda fountain and an old-fashioned popcorn wagon that looked as if it had had a lot of use.

"This is . . . something," she said, momentarily distracted.

"It's also soundproof."

At the foot of the aisle, Ben halted abruptly and turned her to face him. They were still holding hands. Carrie felt a tremor in his. A vein had popped out in his forehead, and his breathing sounded labored. Was he angry enough, she wondered, to have a heated argument right here in his best friend's house?

Despite the soundproofing, he spoke in a hoarse whisper. "You asked me a question."

Carrie tried to draw away, but he held onto her hand. Her skin went so icy that it burned. She desperately wanted to crawl under something, and couldn't bring herself to meet his gaze.

"Say it again, Caroline."

She wasn't sure she could. Her throat had closed up. She cleared it a couple of times, and finally mouthed, "Are you in love with me?" The words scalded her.

Ben released her hand. Carrie stood her ground because she was afraid her legs wouldn't carry her to the emergency exit, much less all the way up the sloping center aisle to the door through which they had entered.

She stared at his chest and waited, terrified that she was about to hear Ben say no—terrified even more that Price Carmichael's attorney might say yes.

Moving closer, he tucked a finger under her chin, forcing Carrie to tilt back her head and look him in the face. For the eternity of a held breath, he studied Carrie's hair and eyes and lips in almost scientific detail, the knotted muscles in his jaw working fitfully beneath the skin. His shuttered expression gradually opened and softened.

"Let's go," she managed, tears stinging her eyes.

Ben slowly shook his head.

"Please," she whispered, a tear sliding from her eye.

He caught the tear on the tip of a thumb, then slid his fingers into Carrie's hair, cradling her face as if it were a fragile soap bubble that might burst at the slightest pressure.

"Am I in love with Caroline Washburn?" he murmured as if to himself.

Lowering his head, Ben kissed her with aching tenderness. Carrie felt herself floating, drifting, as more tears streamed down her flushed cheeks. Their lips parted just long enough for him to repeat his words, sounding more like a statement than a question this time, but still giving no proper answer.

His arms slid around her, pulling her close. She felt his smile as they kissed again, her hands flat against his chest, tuned in to the silent thunder of his racing heartbeat. She felt lost and confused and more alive than she had ever been in her life.

She wanted the moment to never end.

She wanted reality to never return.

She wanted the utter peace of never hearing the word no.

Through closed lids, Carrie dimly sensed lights blinking.

Off. On. Off. On.

Her first thought was that her brain must be shorting out, overloaded as it was by the cascade of electrical sensations coursing through her body. Gradually, very gradually, she progressed to a rather sketchy recollection that a storm was raging outside, unheard in the soundproof environs of the theater.

Opening her eyes with great reluctance, she realized the lights were blinking off and on in an unnaturally steady rhythm. Ben seemed to reach that awareness at about the same time. Their lips parted, leaving Carrie's feeling cold and abandoned. Together, they looked up the aisle toward the hallway door to the figure leaning casually against the doorjamb, her hand on the light switches.

"Trish," Ben said, a gravely edge in his voice, "don't you know how to knock?"

"Really, Benjie . . . on a soundproof door?" Trish's smile became a grin. "Actually, I did clear my throat before I looked. But I guess you didn't hear."

Carrie felt herself blush deeply from head to toe. She was still wrapped up in Ben's arms, and he showed no inclination to let her go. *Lovesick.* The words now had the clear ring of a tolling bell. He still hadn't said that he was in love with her. But he certainly had been behaving as if he might be.

If only Trish hadn't intruded.

"Have we been missed?" Carrie asked, surprised by the calm clarity in her voice, so utterly at odds with the emotions rampaging inside her.

"Oh, not that I've noticed." Trish looked from Carrie to Ben and back again, her eyes shining as if she had discovered a pirate's treasure chest.

Ben made a growling sound deep in his throat. Keeping Carrie tucked firmly under one arm, he took a step or two up the aisle toward their hostess. Trish smiled and frowned at the same time, as if she regretted having barged in on them.

"So sorry, Carrie," she said. "But Ben seems to have an urgent phone call."

Carrie felt him tense.

"Who is it?" he asked.

"Someone called Simeon Potts." Trish held up a cellular phone. "I took the liberty of answering your cell. The kitchen helper found it under the dining table. It must have fallen out of your pocket at dinner."

"What?" His hands shot to his pants' pockets.

Carrie gave Ben a quizzical look that he barely acknowledged. Without a word, he turned and planted

Calypso Wind

a quick peck on the top of her head, then bounded up the aisle to snatch his cell phone from Trish's outstretched hand.

At the door, he glanced back at Carrie. Their gazes locked just long enough for her to register the oddly predatory gleam in his eyes. Then he was gone.

Trish stared after him as he trotted off down the hallway. Then she looked down the aisle at Carrie. "What on earth was all that about?"

"I have no idea." Carrie said.

Which was a half-truth, because something about that parting look in Ben's eyes had left Carrie with a distinct impression that the phone call had something to do with her.

With the screening room door open, she could hear the storm rumbling away outside. Long after Trish excused herself and returned to her other guests, letting the soundproof door drift shut, Carrie stood alone, hugging herself.

Down in the front row, the velour-upholstered aisle seat rocked slightly when Carrie settled into it. She sat there for a moment, staring at the blank projection screen in front of her, then pushed on the chair's armrests. The backrest tilted back and a footrest popped up beneath her legs. Trying to relax the tension in her body, she closed her eyes in the vacuum-like silence and waited.

Time crawled.

Eventually, time seemed to come to a standstill. Silence, broken only by the restless scratching of her fingernails on a small black-enamel tray attached to the right armrest, became a colorless, odorless weight pressing down on her mind. Straining under the invisible burden, her thoughts grew sluggish even as her emotions began to feel crushed and bruised.

But through it all, the memory of Ben's kiss lingered, as fresh and real as if their lips had never parted. He had never told her if he loved her. Even so, the tenderness of his kiss had sealed her ever-growing love for him as surely as if he had tattooed himself on her soul. The question that preyed on Carrie's mind now was, had she gone and fallen in love with kind, gentle, trustworthy Ben Ross or with Price Carmichael's lawyer? Because she knew in her heart that she could trust her love with only one of them.

Some while later, the door behind her at the top of the aisle finally opened with a sound that was remarkably like a gasp.

Ben slouched down the aisle with his hands in his pockets, showing none of the energized spirit that had sent him bolting out the door earlier. Looking preoccupied, he stepped past Carrie with hardly a glance at her and dropped into the next seat. Shoving the chair into recliner position, he folded his hands across his belt and stared hard at the blank projection screen in front of them. Stared *through* the screen, if appearances meant anything.

Carrie gave him two full minutes before speaking. "That must have been one very disappointing phone call."

He tilted his head first to the left, then the right, then sighed. "Not disappointing," he said at last. "Just . . . inconclusive."

His reticence puzzled Carrie. This time, her patience held together for barely thirty seconds. "Ben, are you acting dumb for the sake of mystery, or to keep from lying to me?"

He rolled his head on the backrest and looked at her, a frown line creasing his forehead. "Carrie, I've never once come within shouting distance of lying to you about anything."

She wanted to believe him—found that she *did* believe him. But she still wasn't satisfied. "Then you won't mind saying whether the call had anything to do with me."

His paused long enough to leave the impression that he was carefully considering his options before answering. "Indirectly," he said.

"Define indirectly, please."

His chest swelled, then deflated. "Let's not get into this right now, okay?"

Ben extended a hand to her, palm up, a gentle plea in his eyes. Carrie wanted to take it, to just let the matter slide. But there was a lot more at stake than how much she cared for Ben. It was evident that he was holding out on her about something. How could she even begin to fully trust him—to trust that Ben Ross was of a higher order than Price Carmichael—if he couldn't trust her as much as she trusted him?

"Sorry, Ben." She sat up straight and took his hand in both of hers. "But this is the second time in less than an hour that I've felt like the subject of some kind of conspiracy. Call it paranoia, but I don't like the idea that people are doing things behind my back just because they think it's for my own good."

"Even if it *is* for your good?"

She couldn't help bristling. "I'm not a child, Ben. No matter how good your intentions are, it isn't right for you or Trish or anyone else to be trying to arrange my life without even bothering to consult me."

"Nobody's arranging your life, Carrie." Ben threw himself out of the chair and paced the width of the screening room. "I just don't want to see you hurt."

"Hurt? Ben, what on earth are you talking about?"

Halting in front of her, he jammed his hands back into his pockets and stared down at his shoes. His jaw muscles were knotted again. Carrie had been so deeply engaged in a private war with her emotions that she hadn't noticed until now that Ben appeared to have a battle royal going with himself.

"You're right, Carrie. I have no license to look out for your best interests unless you ask me to." His gaze lifted long enough to catch her eye before returning to the floor, as if he knew she wasn't going to like what he had to say next. "The call was from a private security expert I hired yesterday. Simeon Potts, from Kingston."

Before Carrie could get in a word, Ben quickly went on to describe how he had leaked word around Calypso Beach that he was in the habit of leaving valuables lying around his suite. The gold Rolex that Carrie had returned to him earlier, a cutting-edge laptop computer and other high-tech equipment . . . you name it. He had made sure the scuttlebutt was that he rarely bothered securing the items in the resort's safe.

"I don't understand." Carrie couldn't believe he would be so negligent. "Why would you do that when you know rooms are being burglarized?"

"Simeon has my room staked out."

She sat dumbstruck for a moment. "Ben, don't tell me you're using yourself as bait."

"Nope. Just my suite." He spread both hands wide and smiled. "As you can see, I'm right here, safe and sound."

Carrie leaned forward, elbows on her knees, and steepled her hands in front of her face. This was the last thing she had expected. "But why would you—"

"The phone call was Simeon letting me know that Sybil and Arnold Rodgers have cancelled an outing they'd signed up for just this morning. They seem to do that a lot—bailing out of excursions at the last minute and staying put at the resort."

"It's stormy this evening," Carrie reminded him. "Lots of guests probably chose to stay in."

Ben looked skeptical. "Their scheduled excursion was a pricey dinner and historical experience over at Rose Hall. And the sign-up fee, as you undoubtedly know, was nonrefundable."

Carrie had completely forgotten about the special historical tour and candlelight dinner at the old Rose Hall mansion. "Rain or shine, it wouldn't be like Sybil and Arnold to miss out on something like that," she conceded. "Not unless one of them got sick."

He gave a single deep nod and aimed a finger at her, as if she had made his point for him. "According to Simeon, the pair is porking out in the Calypso Beach Brasserie as we speak."

She scratched her nose, which was suddenly itching like crazy.

"But why focus on them?" she asked.

The fact was that Sybil and Arnold were the only names that Carrie had penciled in on her own list of possible suspects at the moment. But that little detail was overridden by a burst of defensiveness for the hapless couple. As it happened, she liked them a lot.

"Simple," Ben said. "It's a matter of opportunity, which is something Sybil and Arnold Rodgers have had in abundance. As I said, one or the other of them seems to cancel out on a lot of excursions. Tonight, it was both. And Simeon checked around—they ship a whole crate of stuff back to the States every two or three days."

"They have eleven grandchildren, Ben."

Calypso Wind

"Still, whole crates. That's a lot of souvenir T-shirts."

Carrie reluctantly gave Ben's premise the consideration it deserved. Certainly, he wasn't alone in wondering about Arnold and Sybil. From time to time, the idea that those two old people might be pulling the wool over everyone's eyes had rolled around in the back of her own mind. But now that it came down to saying it right out loud, she found that she couldn't call them thieves.

Maybe she was being naive. But at the end of the day, she felt lucky to know two such generous, good-hearted people.

"You're wrong about Arnold and Sybil," she said. "I'm positive."

"You are?" Ben looked as if he'd just stumbled against a brick wall that he hadn't been aware existed.

Carrie was flattered that he apparently gave so much credence to her opinion of the old couple.

He shoved his hands back into his pockets and scowled at the floor.

"Well, I don't suppose it matters," he said. "Simeon is watching from across the hall. If the thief—whoever that may be—breaks in, it'll be their last roundup."

He returned to pacing, hands clasped behind his back, placing one foot in front of the other in a slow march to nowhere.

Carrie watched until she grew restless herself. She caught up with him near the emergency exit.

"Ben, why are you doing this?" she asked again, putting a hand on his arm to stop him. "Why go to the trouble and expense of setting this up and staking out your room back at the resort?"

"I'm doing it for you, naturally," he said, as if nothing could be simpler. Resting both hands on her shoulders, he pressed his lips briefly to her forehead. "Do you have any idea what being even remotely connected to a scandal could do to your reputation? I'm not about to let that happen."

His tenderness caused a sharp pain to blossom in Carrie's chest, making breathing difficult. She had been on her own for so long now, scrabbling through her days and nights with no one to share her heart. Then along came Ben Ross and threw open a window.

More than anything, she wanted to lean into Ben and feel his arms close around her again. She wanted to slip into the dream of loving him—and being loved by a man who drew dogs and cats and birds and babies like steel filings to a magnet. She wanted to spend the rest of her life taking moonlit walks with this man, soaking up his magic.

But a shadow had crept into the room, and she couldn't make it go away.

When she finally spoke, her voice sounded strained. "This is the way it would always be, isn't it?"

Ben gave her a questioning look.

"If I ever signed on the dotted line and became a card-carrying Carmichael like you want," she said quietly, "you'd always be there doing the right thing."

He studied her intently, as if he must be missing something. "That's right," he said. "Is there something wrong with my wanting to look out for you?"

"Look out for me?" Even as she reached out a trembling hand and touched his chest, she felt new distance spreading between them. "Oh, Ben. I have this terrible feeling that your first priority would always be to protect the precious Carmichael name, at any cost. You'd always want to be there at the controls." Carrie had struggled too hard for her own identity to agree to that.

He started to speak, but she cut him off.

"I guess I don't blame you for being so loyal to my uncle," she said. "Sam told me how much the man meant to you, and why."

Ben frowned.

"Please, don't go getting upset with Sam," she said. "He was just being your friend."

Carrie pressed her hand more firmly to Ben's chest, taking strength from the feel of his steady heartbeat. Fair was fair, she thought. Sam Rivers had revealed secrets about his friend's past that Ben might have preferred to keep locked away. She felt that she could no longer keep Ben in the dark about her own family history, especially now that she knew he had been so much a part of Price Carmichael's life.

She lifted her chin and looked him in the eye. "Ben, I've come to realize that secrets can fester. I'm afraid . . . I don't want the truth to hurt you." *Or to hurt us . . . if there is an us.* "But it's time that you knew what Price Carmichael meant to Mom and me. And why."

His lips tightened—keen interest coupled with wariness. Carrie took his hands, holding on as she held his gaze. At one time, before she had come to know and love Ben, she might have taken pleasure in opening his eyes. But now the prospect of causing him pain was a hot skewer twisting inside her.

There was nothing fair about the truth hurting so much. But for the life of her, she couldn't see a way around it.

"Have you ever seen a picture of my mother?" she asked.

He shook his head, watching her carefully.

"She was so beautiful." Carrie sighed in remembrance, her chin bunching. She swallowed to loosen her tight throat. "And warm and funny. She had enough love in her to mother ten kids, and I think she wanted that many, but I was the only one to show up at her party. So she gave me ten times the love that probably most kids get, and still had enough kindness left over to spread around to friends and any lost soul who came along. She was a treasure to everyone who knew her. I still miss her every single day."

"I'm sorry," Ben said with sincerity. "I would like to have met her."

Carrie smiled crookedly. "That means a lot to me, Ben. Because, you see, that's a fundamental difference between you and Uncle Price. I think you wouldn't

Calypso Wind 195

have tried to change Mom into something she wasn't. You would have accepted her for the wonderful, incredibly good-hearted person she was."

He shifted his feet, looking uneasy, as if sensing that she was about to tell him something he might not want to hear. That made it difficult for Carrie to go on. But she had come this far, and there was no going back.

"Mom was a late baby, almost twenty years younger than Uncle Price," Carrie began. "By the time she was nineteen and a freshman in college, he had already taken over as head of the family. That was fine, until Mom fell in love with a fireman she met at a community fundraiser. Have you heard about this?"

Ben shook his head again, frowning.

"Well, Uncle Price had a fit when he found out that his kid sister was seeing someone so far beneath her station in life, as he put it. I guess maybe he had in mind that he would marry her off to the scion of some other rich family. Mom tried to explain to him that Mike Washburn was the love of her life, her soul mate, but he wouldn't hear of it. Worse, he threatened to disown her if they didn't stop seeing each other at once."

Carrie took a deep breath and spilled out the rest. "Mike Washburn tried to break it off for Mom's sake. He told her he'd never be able to give her a big house and a fancy car. He even tried to make a joke of it, saying he'd look like a complete fool in a tuxedo, and wouldn't know caviar from kettle scrapings. But Mom told me he had tears in his eyes when he said it."

Tears brimmed in Carrie's eyes. She heard her mother's gentle voice in her head, telling the story that she had repeated to Carrie so many times that it had seemed more like a fairy tale than reality. Looking back now, it seemed as if she had been trying to transmit to Carrie some deeper truth that she intended for her daughter to take with her through life as a guiding principle.

"Mom knew her own heart, Ben. And she trusted her soul mate's character, so she didn't just stand by and let Mike do what he thought was best for her. She did what she *knew* was best for both of them. She told Mike that caviar was nothing but a bunch of smelly fish eggs. She warned him that if he ever so much as tried on a tux, she would skin him alive. Then she packed a bag, climbed into his old rattletrap, and ran away with him."

The rest came out in two sentences strained between opposite emotions, like water gushing from hot and cold faucets.

"Mom and Dad had a gloriously happy marriage right up until the day he died, and she cherished every moment of the nine years they had together. But Uncle Price lived up to his word—he never spoke to his baby sister again."

Ben didn't utter a word for a moment. Then he stepped back and raked his fingers slowly back through his hair, his eyes darting rapidly from side to side as if searching for something.

"Uncle Price never forgave Mom for running off and living happily ever after," Carrie went on. "She told me

Calypso Wind

she wrote him letters, first every week, then monthly, and finally every year at Christmas. But he never answered them—never even read them for all anyone knows. But I think Mom tried her best to love him anyway, even if it was from afar."

Tears coursed down Carrie's cheeks. She didn't cry often, and was embarrassed that she was doing so in front of Ben again. Worse, she knew she had wounded him with her awful truth about his idol, and that double-edged sword cut her deeply.

She took a conciliatory step toward him, but Ben had already started turning away with the sluggish movements of a sleepwalker. She let him go, though that hurt her, too.

"I'm sorry." She was aware that she was echoing his words of a moment earlier. "It's just . . . you're so much like Price Carmichael, Ben. You can't abide anything being beyond your control."

There—she had gotten it all out. In the process, her stomach had gone hollow, and all the oxygen seemed to have been squeezed from the air.

Ben kept clawing at his hair, worrying it into a tangle as complex as Carrie's own snarled emotions.

Minutes crawled by, as silent as a pent up breath in the soundproof screening room. Carrie held icy fingers to her lips, wishing she could take it all back—knowing that every word had needed to be said.

"I'm sorry," Carrie whispered once more. "I wish . . ."

I wish . . .

She couldn't finish the thought. Because when it came right down to the bedrock of loving Ben Ross, it seemed too much as if she were wishing upon a star, hoping for a fairy tale. She envisioned a small brick house on a quiet street, with toys on the lawn. The man she loved sprawled in a recliner reading the Saturday newspaper, surrounded by kids and dogs and cats, with Carrie standing in the doorway smiling at it all.

The image came to her in a rush so vivid that she let out a small cry that choked in her throat.

The vision evaporated, leaving behind the reality that Ben's mission in life had to do with mansions and riches and a name that Carrie simply could never live with.

She turned and rushed up the aisle toward the door.

Price turned his back on his own sister. Ben stood flat-footed, shaken. Not for one instant had it occurred to him not to believe Carrie's version of what had transpired all those years ago. If he had learned one thing since coming down to Jamaica, it was that Carrie Washburn was honesty personified.

He took a clumsy step, feeling as if he were wading through hip-deep rubble. Everything he had lived for—worked for—since the day he met Price Carmichael suddenly seemed—false. He had spent nearly a third of his life idolizing a man who was capable of disowning

Calypso Wind 199

his only sister, and over what? *Status. Social standing. The status quo.*

And now, the one beacon of pure integrity that Ben knew of was fleeing up the aisle in tears.

"Carrie!" His voice rasped. He finally got his legs moving and bolted after her. "Carrie . . . wait!"

At the sound of his voice, she broke into a run. Ben caught her at the door and whirled her around, pulling her into his arms. She felt like a wooden statue . . . a shivering wooden statue.

"I've been a blind fool," he said. "I didn't even know you existed until Price's will surfaced. And then I just naturally assumed too much, and wrongly."

He was breathing hard, his pulse pounding in his ears. Everything had come tumbling down so fast, he couldn't seem to regain his equilibrium. But something in him sensed that he held balance and reason in his arms. The longer he stood there hanging onto Carrie, the more that certainty grew, along with another that said if he ever let her go, he might never get her back.

"Sweet, sweet Carrie," he murmured into her strawberry-scented hair. "Can we start over? Will you give me another chance?"

Her shivering became a shudder. Ben felt her tears soaking through the front of his shirt. He took her face in his hands and tilted it up so he could see her. She was so beautiful, with her cheeks flushed and her eyes turned to liquid. Just looking at her squeezed a fist around his heart.

He leaned down and brushed her lips with his. Carrie sucked in a breath that stole his.

"The more I know you," he whispered hoarsely, then corrected himself, "the more I understand you, the more I love you for what you are—not what I wanted you to be."

Her lips quivered. "Love?"

He nodded, stunned to hear himself saying the words. "Yes . . . a thousand times yes. I love you, Carrie Washburn. And if you could bring yourself to love me back despite the unmitigated fool I've been. . . ."

She hiccupped, then melted into his arms with a wet bubble of laughter. He squeezed her so tightly that she struggled, gasping for breath. He loosened his grip just enough so she could look up at him with sparkling eyes.

He bent and kissed her long and tenderly. When she kissed him back, with a little hum of unbridled pleasure in her throat, a surge of euphoria washed over Ben. A moment earlier, he had been a drowning man. Now, suddenly, he stood on top of the world.

After awhile, he stood her away from him a little and gazed into her eyes. She looked as dazed as he felt.

"Listen to me, Carrie, this is a promise. No more working behind your back," he grinned sheepishly "for your own good. I'll call Simeon and tell him to go home. We'll let the resort handle the problem of those burglaries. How does that sound?"

Carrie grinned back, like the sun rising on a brand new morning. "That sounds like the man I love."

Ben reached into his pocket for his cell phone and auto-dialed a number without looking. While Simeon's cell phone rang, he stole another kiss.

Chapter Thirteen

The storm had passed, leaving the road strewn with twigs and leaf litter. They hardly spoke during the drive back to Calypso Beach. They had reached a point where words didn't seem necessary. Carrie sat close to Ben, feeling as if a different kind of storm had passed, leaving the two of them shaken to the core, but washed clean and safe.

Better than safe, she thought.

The headlights cut through the darkness ahead. Without taking his gaze off the road, Ben reached over and took her hand. He pressed the back of her hand to his lips, then placed it on her lap and gave it a little pat before returning his own hand to the steering wheel.

"This is going to take some adjustment, you know," he said.

Carrie looked up at him. He had seemed deep in thought as they drove along. And yet his statement felt out of the blue. "Loving someone is difficult for you?"

"No, no." He smiled contentedly. "In fact, I'm finding that quite easy. Irresistible, in fact."

"Then what?"

Ben sucked in his lower lip.

A full quarter of a mile later, he said, "I guess I've never been used to *being* loved. It requires—concessions."

"Like sharing the controls?"

He took his attention off the road just long enough to wink at her, straight-faced. "Like that."

With a laugh, Carrie snuggled her head against his shoulder. "I'll help you get used to that."

Ben chuckled. "I'll just bet you will."

The silence closed in again, broken only by the sound of the car engine and the sibilant rush of night air past the windows.

Carrie decided that she would just have to get used to his intermittent silences—the nothing-sound of Ben in deep thought. Eventually, she was confident he would get around to sharing those thoughts with her.

The lobby was quiet as Ben approached the front desk with Carrie tucked under his arm. The drowsy night clerk glanced up from the newspaper he was reading, and slid off his stool. Ben asked if he had any messages. The clerk yawned and stretched before rummaging around under the desk and coming up with a single pink slip.

After quickly scanning the message, Ben frowned and slipped it into his pocket.

"Something wrong?" Carrie asked.

"Not really." He shook his head. "Just a note from Simeon. Since his services are no longer required, he's planning to go ahead and head back down to Kingston tonight."

"So . . . why the frown?"

"Oh, I just liked my plan for trapping a burglar. But what the devil . . . it might not have worked out anyway."

As they crossed the lobby toward the elevator bank, Carrie looped an arm around his waist. Now that Ben had given up his crazy scheme just to please her, she caught herself wondering if she had been right to object. And there was another consideration that bothered her.

"You've already put the word out that you leave valuables in your room," she said. "Nobody has sprung the trap. So aren't you still in danger of being burglarized, with or without Simeon watching?"

Ben put on a smile and kissed the top of her head. "Not to worry, sweetheart. All my valuables are stowed away safely in the resort's safe."

"But still—"

"If it'll make you happy, I'll tape a sign on my door saying it was all a joke."

"This isn't funny, Ben."

"I don't know. Seems like it ought to be."

At the elevators, Ben pressed a knuckle against the "up" button. While they waited, Carrie glanced out through the open archway at the swimming pool deck. The flagstones were still damp from the storm.

Most of the deck lights had been turned off for the night. But in the murky glow from the pool lights, she spotted Arnold and Sybil Rodgers seated alone at one of the tables. They were nearly lost in the shadows, almost as if they didn't want to be seen.

An elevator door glided open.

Ben nudged Carrie toward the elevator. But at the last second, she stepped back.

"You go ahead, Ben." She touched his arm. "I see Arnold and Sybil outside. It's awfully late. Guess I'd better check and see if anything's wrong."

Ben followed her gaze through the archway. "I'll wait."

He's still suspicious of them, Carrie thought. She didn't want to admit that she was too, just a little.

"No, really, go ahead up to your room," she said. "You're tired. Besides, I'd better run a routine check on the other Galaxy clients anyway. Make sure they've all made it back from their evening out." It wouldn't do to find out in the morning that some of them had been stranded by the storm.

"Carrie, my dearest darling, I am going to escort you to your room," he insisted, bending to peck her on the nose.

"Oh, you don't know how much I appreciate the sentiment, my love, but I have a job to do." Carrie threw her arms around Ben's neck and stood on tiptoe to plant a kiss on his chin. Then she unceremoniously pushed him backwards into the elevator. "Besides, bozo, this might be a good time for you to practice taking your hands off the controls."

He growled. Carrie growled back, waggling her fingers at him. After she turned away, she felt him watching her right up until the elevator door glided shut. She glowed all the way across the lobby to the pool deck.

Arnold and Sybil looked her way as she stepped outside. They appeared a little embarrassed, as if Carrie had interrupted something. She noticed too late that the elderly couple was holding hands, and realized that she had barged in on a romantic interlude under the stars.

"I'm just checking to make sure all's well," Carrie said, hanging back.

"All's perfectly well dear," said a dreamy-eyed Sybil.

"In fact," added Arnold, peering out at the moonlit beach, "now that the storm has passed, perfection could take lessons from this night."

You are so right, Carrie thought, wishing she had let Ben wait for her. A walk on the tropical beach under the stars would have been so . . .

"Mark waited up for you."

Sybil's words jolted Carrie out of her brief reverie. "Oh?"

"I suppose he was worried about you being out in that storm." Sybil glanced back into the lobby, then gave Carrie a knowing look. "But we noticed you had someone to look after you."

"Now, now, Syb." Arnold shook a crooked finger at his wife. "Don't be joshing the girl."

"Well, Ben Ross does seem like a fine, upstanding young man," Sybil said.

"You know his name?" Carrie was surprised. She didn't recall ever having introduced them to Ben.

"Why, of course," Arnold said. "Everybody's been asking around. He's attracted a lot of attention, the way every dog on the beach tags after him like he's their pack leader. And I heard a waiter over at the Sand Dollar talking about an incident with their birds the other evening. Your beau seems to have quite interesting qualities."

Yes, he most definitely does, Carrie thought.

"Did, uhm, you enjoy the excursion to Rose Hall Mansion this evening?" she asked, fishing, and not wanting them to know that someone had been keeping tabs on them.

The couple's demeanor abruptly changed. Sybil's hands knotted in her lap, and Arnold wiped a hand across his suddenly furrowed brow. They both looked shaken. Carrie took notice, fearing that she might have been wrong about them.

Sybil murmured something that Carrie didn't quite catch. She moved closer to the old woman. "I'm sorry?"

"We didn't go to Rose Hall," Sybil said.

"Really?" Unwise though it probably was, Carrie couldn't help offering them an excuse. "I guess the storm kept a lot of guests in."

Arnold shook his head, then laughed dryly. "Not us. You see, we had an emergency call from home. Our son was reportedly in a terrible automobile accident."

Carrie gasped. "Oh, no!"

"Not to worry, dear," Sybil said quickly. "Gerald is fine. It was a case of mistaken identity. He was safely home eating supper with his family at the time of the accident. Fortunately, the real driver of the car is going to be all right. But let me tell you, it was a horrific fright for Arnie and me until it all got straightened out."

"I can imagine."

"We were so relieved that we came down here to sit in the moonlight."

"And canoodle," Arnie added.

Sybil gave a hoot of laughter and swatted at him. "You are incorrigible."

"Well, I'm glad all is well," Carrie said.

She chatted with the Rodgers for a little while longer before going back inside to check with the night clerk. Most of the Galaxy clients had been by to pick up their room key-cards. The clerk was kind enough not to mention that the whole kit and caboodle of Galaxy Tours would be checking out first thing in the morning . . . and good riddance to the thief among them.

As she turned away from the desk, a prickly sensa-

Calypso Wind 209

tion crept across her shoulders. She scanned the lobby, convinced that someone was watching her. But except for the clerk, and Sybil and Arnold out on the pool deck, not a living soul was in sight.

Ben had suspected the Rodgerses of the burglaries. Carrie wondered if he had worried about her talking with them out there alone, and had come back down to keep an eye on her. She didn't know whether to smile or frown at that thought. She liked feeling protected, but if Ben still had control issues . . .

Carrie took the elevator up to her floor and wandered down the hushed corridor to Lana's room. She tapped lightly on the door, in case Lana was already in bed. The greater likelihood was that Lana was out on the town, no matter that her business was collapsing around her ears.

Getting no response, Carrie sighed, and moved on to her own room.

Midnight had come and gone some time ago. As exciting as her evening had been, she was exhausted. Her brain felt like a fuzzball, her eyes burned, and her new shoes seemed to have shrunken at least a size. She looked forward to sliding between the sheets of her bed and dreaming of Ben. Sweet, tender dreams, they would be, if she didn't lie awake all night replaying the pleasure of his embrace over and over.

She slid her key-card into the lock and opened the door.

Across the room, the sliding door to the balcony was

open a crack, the sheer curtains wafting slightly in the breeze. Carrie thought she had closed that door before leaving that evening, but shrugged it off as the tropical night air seduced her thoughts back to the walk she had taken with Ben at the Rivers estate.

She closed her eyes. Inhaling the heady scent of tropical flowers, she resurrected the feeling of Ben's strong arms around her . . . the tenderness of his kiss . . . the feathery stroke of a cat's tail against her leg.

That last drew a soft laugh as she switched on the light.

"Wha—"

The room looked as if a hurricane had struck. The floral spread was torn from the bed, the mattress thrown half off the box springs. Every drawer in the dresser was pulled open, her clothes strewn on the floor. Near the door to the balcony, her rolling suitcase lay open on its side, the lining slashed. Through the open door to the adjoining bathroom, she could see her toiletries scattered on the tile floor.

For a long moment, Carrie couldn't move. She simply stared at the destruction, thunderstruck that she had been victimized by the resort burglar. There was some slim consolation in the thief having found nothing of value, for the simple reason that she owned nothing worth stealing. From the looks of her room, the intruder had been infuriated by that discovery.

Her mind finally unlocked enough for Carrie to wonder why the resort burglar would have chosen her room

Calypso Wind   211

at all. She wasn't a rich tourist, and she was staying in the cheapest room in the resort. That should have been evident to the burglar.

She realized that this was a third piece in a series of imponderables. First, there were the series of burglaries themselves, coming during Galaxy's previous and current visits to Calypso Beach. Add to that the incident where Ben's rented moped had been run over outside the little shop out in the countryside. Now someone had broken in and torn Carrie's luggage and modest traveling wardrobe to smithereens.

As the shock wore off, she moved farther into the room, fists pressed to her lips, straining to put the pieces together. The burglaries occurred during Galaxy's visits . . . then the moped that she had been riding was destroyed . . . and now her room. Each incident had been more personally connected to Carrie, as if a predator were spiraling ever closer.

Carrie halted and slowly lowered her hands.

A shaky breath escaped her. *I'm the common denominator. But why?* Her mind raced. What did she have that anyone . . . *anyone* would want?

Nothing. Not one blessed thing.

Unless you sign the inheritance contract and become Caroline Carmichael.

"Oh, no . . ."

She lunged for the phone on the nightstand and punched in Ben's suite number. The phone rang twice before he picked up, sounding groggy. She had awakened him. She felt a twinge of regret before realizing just how stupid that was, because it couldn't have been him watching her down in the lobby after all.

"Ben, I—"

"Carrie, what is it?" He sounded fully alert now.

"While we were gone, my room was trashed," she blurted. "I think I'm getting this figured out."

"One sec . . ."

She clutched the phone, listening to rustling sounds. The snick of a zipper. Ben was throwing on clothes. Before she knew it, he would be at her door. She wouldn't mind one little bit. Carrie reached down and picked up the butterfly blouse he had given her. A dirty shoe print marked one sleeve. She had never felt more alone.

Ben came back on the line, his voice barely audible. "Uh . . . Carrie, you aren't calling from my bathroom by any chance?"

Carrie looked at the phone. "Calling from your *what*?"

"Didn't think so."

She heard a soft thump, as if he had placed his receiver on a hard surface. "Ben?"

Then, seconds later, a much louder thump, like a door banging back against a wall, followed by scuffling sounds.

"Ben, what's going on?"

The scuffling intensified, accompanied by assorted grunts and crashes. When she heard glass break, Carrie threw down the phone and bolted for the door.

Calypso Wind 213

Racing up the hallway, she skidded to a halt and banged the flat of her hand against the door to Lana's room, praying that she had been wrong and that Lana wasn't still out on the town after all. She kept hammering away loud enough to awaken the entire floor until at last the door flew open. Lana stood in a silky robe, a jar of cold cream in one hand, a wad of tissues in the other, her makeup half off.

"Emergency!" Carrie cried, too frightened to explain. She grabbed her boss and dragged her toward the elevators at a dead run.

The elevators were too slow. Carrie and Lana took the stairs down, reaching Ben's floor out of breath.

"Are you going to tell me what this is all about?" Lana trotted alongside Carrie, still holding the jar of cold cream while dabbing at her face with the tissues.

Too frantic to respond, Carrie tore down the hallway to Ben's suite. She had just begun pounding a fist on the door when two uniformed resort security guards rounded the corner at the end of the hallway, coming from the direction of the elevators. Seeing the commotion ahead, the guards charged toward them.

"Here, now," one of them shouted, "what's the problem?"

They made a grab for Carrie, but Lana threw herself in their way. "Leave her alone," she barked. "Can't you see this is an emergency?"

"Someone's attacking Ben!" Carrie jerked off a shoe and held it up like a weapon.

Lana gaped at Carrie. The two guards looked at each other.

"Don't just stand there," Carrie cried. "Break down the door!"

The guards hesitated, then one of them took out a devise that he slipped into the key-card slot. In an instant, the lock deactivated. He pushed open the door, and the guards stepped inside, one after the other.

Carrie followed them into the sitting room.

The room was empty. And silent. The guards turned and gave both Carrie and Lana a skeptical look. Ignoring them, and terrified by the stillness, Carrie hobbled toward the bedroom, her shoe held high.

She found Ben leaning against the wall on the far side of the bed, shirtless and barefooted, panting. One side of his jaw was turning dark red as if a bruise were coming on. Eyeing the shoe in Carrie's hand, he grinned crookedly.

"It's okay, sweetheart," he said. "I took care of him all by myself."

Lightheaded with relief, Carrie put the shoe back on and edged around the end of the bed to have a look.

Mark Hanes lay curled at Ben's feet, both arms clutching his stomach, a dazed look in his eyes. He had apparently had the wind knocked out of him. His mouth opened and closed like a beached fish as he gulped for air.

The security guards shouldered into the room. They took one look at the scene, and then one of them quickly made a call on a small radio device clipped to the lapel of his jacket. His partner came over and hauled Mark into a sitting position, handcuffing him before propping him against the wall.

Ben slumped down onto the corner of the bed. "Whew! The adrenaline rush just left me."

Easing down next to him, Carrie touched the darkening bruise on his jaw. He winced, and shifted her hand from his jaw to his chest, wrapping his other arm around her.

"How did Mark get in?" she asked.

"By way of the balcony," said one of the guards, who had briefly stepped outside. "A rope is hanging down from the floor above."

She peeked over at Mark, who seemed to be coming around. He shifted against the wall, realized he was handcuffed, and a look of panic settled in.

"I never in this world would have believed Mark was the burglar," Carrie murmured to herself.

Lana materialized with a damp washrag, which she folded against Ben's jaw. He held it in place, and the three of them sat side by side waiting for the emotional dust to settle. Every now and then, one or the other of them would glance over at Mark, whose fearful gaze danced around the room without once coming near them.

Within what seemed like a very short time, Henry Matalon came striding into the room. The head of Resort Security eyed the threesome seated on the bed.

Then, without a word, he stepped over and glowered down at Mark Hanes, handcuffed on the floor. Matalon shoved back his sports coat and put his hands on his hips, shaking his head.

One of the security guards motioned for Matalon to check out the balcony. Before he went, Matalon gave Carrie a steady look, then smiled ever so slightly.

"You owe someone an apology," Lana said to him.

"I hope so." Matalon nodded, glancing back and forth between Lana and Carrie. "I do indeed hope so." He left them sitting on the bed and went out onto the balcony to inspect the rope.

After awhile, Carrie felt Ben straighten suddenly. He was staring across the room at his leather attaché case, standing open on a small round table. The contents looked as if they had been rifled. A handful of papers lay scattered on the floor.

Slowly, Ben turned and looked past her again at Mark. "Well, well. Now isn't that interesting?"

"What?" she and Lana asked in unison.

Ben shook his head, his lips twitching until they finally broke out in a smile. "Tell me, Hanes," he said after a moment. "Exactly how are you related to Price Carmichael?"

Mark gave him a sour look. He struggled against the handcuffs, the look of panic returning. Then his shoulders slumped in defeat.

"Second cousin by marriage," he mumbled at the floor.

Calypso Wind

Ben nodded. "I thought so."

It took Carrie a couple of minutes to sort out the significance of that exchange. When she finally did, the pieces to the puzzle suddenly came flying together.

"That's it, isn't it?" she said, though the entire picture wasn't yet clear to her.

"What do you mean, 'that's it?' " Lana shot to her feet, throwing up her hands. "Would someone please tell me what this is all about?"

Carrie waited for Ben to explain it to Lana. When he didn't, she took a shot at it herself. "My uncle left me a lot of money—if I agreed to abide by certain conditions set out in an inheritance contract. The deadline on the contract is this weekend. If I don't sign on, everything goes to distant relatives of my uncle's late wife—Mark apparently being one of them."

She got up and gathered the papers off the floor, placing them neatly in the briefcase. To her surprise, there didn't seem to be a legal document in the bunch.

"The contract is in the resort safe," Ben said. "But Mark didn't know that."

Carrie glanced at the shackled accountant to see how he took that news. Mark lowered his head to his raised knees, taking it badly.

"My guess is that Mark has been burglarizing rooms in an attempt to create a public scandal involving Galaxy Tours," Ben went on. "That would have stained Carrie's reputation, which he must have found out would kill her chance to inherit her uncle's fortune. But that wasn't working . . . at least, not in time. As Carrie said, the deadline for signing is this weekend. It looks like old Mark here got desperate enough to try to steal the contract so Carrie couldn't sign it—or to destroy it if she already had."

"My word, child," Lana eyed Carrie with wonder. "You've inherited a fortune?"

"No, I have not."

Lana sat back down hard on the end of the bed. "Carrie, sweetie, about half of this is going right over my head."

"Well, it gets crazier." Carrie pointed a finger at Mark. "Before he came down that rope he tore up my room first. I bet he was searching for that blasted contract."

Ben lowered the damp cloth, his face flushing in anger. "That's right—your room was broken into."

Carrie nodded.

"You don't know what you're talking about," Mark snapped.

"Oh, yeah?" Ben leaned toward him, his copper-flecked hazel eyes going as cold as sleet. "Then maybe you won't mind telling us what perfectly innocent circumstances led you to shinny down that rope and invade *my* room in the dead of night?" He refolded the damp cloth and pressed it to his jaw. "Not to mention assaulting me."

"You hit me first!"

"And last."

Henry Matalon wandered back into the room, trailed

by the two guards. They appeared to be waiting for something. Then it dawned on Carrie—they were waiting for the police to arrive, of course.

In the twitch of a heartbeat, delayed reaction set in. A tremor started in her fingers and spread rapidly up her arms before slamming down through her body. Ben noticed. He rose as if to embrace her again. But before he could reach her, Carrie whirled away and stumbled out onto the balcony, suddenly suffocating.

The night breeze, still blustery from the storm, tugged at her dress. Carrie leaned against the waist-high railing, wobbly in the knees. The past twenty or so minutes had undone her. She stared down at the moonlit beach, trying to wrench her emotions back under control.

A minute later, the door behind her slid shut. Someone moved to lean next to her against the railing. A hand settled lightly on her bare back.

"Sorry," Ben said. "I wasn't behaving very professionally in there."

She gave a humorless laugh. "There's an official code of conduct for attorneys in this kind of situation?"

"Okay. Let's say I wasn't being very adult."

"How about if we don't say anything at all for awhile?" Her voice shook.

Ben took his hand off her back just when Carrie needed it there most. She held onto the railing for dear life. If she let go, she was afraid she might go spinning off into the night sky.

"I understand," he said, his tone dull with resignation.

"Understand what?" She hadn't meant to sound so brusque. The delayed shock from coming so close—so hideously close—to possibly losing Ben hummed through her body like the forewarning of a major earthquake.

"I understand how nobody in her right mind would want to sign onto this kind of mess." Ben shoved his hands into his pockets and gazed up at the stars. "There really is a limit to what money is worth."

Carrie sucked in her lips and closed her eyes. Ben's acceptance of what was to her a fundamental truth made her want to laugh and cry at the same time. She did neither. The ground she stood on still felt too unstable.

"Mark doesn't seem to think there's a limit," she said.

"Mark is infected with a virulent strain of greed."

Carrie gave herself another minute, then turned and looked at Ben . . . really looked at him. The bruise on his jaw was swelling. He needed an icepack. And she needed to be the one who found one for him. But not quite yet.

"What about you?" she asked. "What's it all worth to J. Benjamin Ross?"

He didn't demean the importance of her question by offering a knee-jerk answer. Instead, he peered past her at the ebony sea, his expression curiously slack, as though waiting for some inner voice to speak for him. Finally, he shook his head.

Calypso Wind 221

"I could have told you just like that," he snapped his fingers, "last week. That's why I came down here. I would have done almost anything to persuade you to sign the inheritance contract."

"And now?"

"Now? As Price Carmichael's attorney, I still believe it's in your best interest to accept everything he left you." He took a deep breath, let it out, and shifted his gaze to Carrie. "But as someone who's deeply in love with you, I would hate to see you—"

Her hand shot up and she pressed her fingers to his lips, cutting him off. *As someone who's deeply in love with you.* The hum in her body became a deeper vibration, like a tuning fork struck inside her heart.

"No, Ben," she whispered. "This isn't about me now. What about you? What happens to you if I don't sign the contract? If my late aunt's distant relatives inherit everything, won't you lose your job?"

Ben cocked his head. "Carrie, no matter who inherits the Carmichael estate, my job is over as soon as the formalities are completed."

"Oh. I thought—"

"You thought I was part of the package? That I had a financial interest in getting you to sign the contract?"

"Well . . ." That was exactly what she had assumed.

He made a whistling sound through the space between his front teeth, looking disgusted at himself. "No way. I should have made that clear from the get-go."

Carrie reached up and touched his jaw. He had gone

through all this not in his own self-interest, but out of a sense of pure duty. *And because he's deeply in love with you. He said so, right out loud.*

"But what happens now?" she asked. "When your work for my uncle is finished?"

Ben took both of her hands in his. "Oh, I don't know. My driving ambition seems to have shifted." He gave her a rueful smile. "Think they could use one more good Yankee lawyer down in Atlanta?"

She stared at him. The vibrating sensation in her chest grew into another full-body tremor. Only this time it was different, carrying no anxiety-ridden sense of suffocation. Carrie hiccupped a laugh that was half sob, beginning to feel as if she had wandered into a dream.

He let go of her hands and cradled her face, his thumbs caressing her cheeks. "I guess I'm doing a lousy job of asking you to marry me, Carrie Washburn."

With another hiccup, she threw her arms around him. Ben held her, rocking gently, stroking her hair. After a long while, he tucked a finger under her chin, lifting her face. Their kiss lingered like an endless sigh, the surf pounding the beach behind them in perfect rhythm with their matched heartbeats.

"I'll follow you anywhere," he said when their lips finally parted.

"Even if you'll be marrying a pauper?"

He studied her face in minute detail, feathering his

fingers along its contours and brushing his lips against the hollows of her temple. He had a peculiar smile that reminded her of their drive back from Sam Rivers's place earlier in the evening.

"You're richer than gold, Precious," he said. "Just being with you forever and ever is all I care about."

"We'll be together." She gazed up at him through a haze of love. "You can take that to the bank."

Chapter Fourteen

"Edmund, please get off my chair," Ben muttered absently, turning away from the late-summer high-rise view of a verdant Boston Common.

The hulking black Labrador bounded down off the desk chair, wagging, his flawed pedigree clearly evident in the lightning-bolt splash of white on his broad chest.

Ben swatted dog hair off the leather upholstery and sat down, frowning anew at the red file folder on the cluttered desk blotter. Always a man of quick decisions, he was amazed that it had taken him almost three months to make up his mind this time.

Once word got out about the foundation, they had been deluged with candidates. Choosing which of them should be the first was one of the hardest things Ben had ever done. He didn't like playing God with other people's lives. But that was precisely what Carrie had been so sure he would be good at.

The intercom giggled. Ben stabbed the button. "What is it, Edna?"

"Incoming!" Edna Kincade piped from the outer office, sounding as giddy as a schoolgirl.

Since last winter, the office had undergone a lot of changes. Ben's secretary wasn't one of the subtle ones. The woman's wardrobe had gone from staid conservative to borderline nutsy since Carrie's arrival in Boston. Edna had even taken to wearing a pink carnation in her hair.

Ben was halfway to the door when Carrie burst in, weighed down with her usual armload of accordion file folders. On this occasion, two gift-wrapped packages balanced precariously on top. Diligently adhering to her pauper status, she wore plain cotton slacks and an oversized yellow T-shirt—oversized because she had scrounged it from the back of his closet during one of her and Edna's packing forays into his apartment.

He appreciated the way Carrie had taken it upon herself to help prepare his move south in the fall. He appreciated everything about Caroline Washburn Carmichael.

You adore everything about her, Ross. You're the luckiest man on the planet.

"Your wardrobe is getting funkier by the week," he said, transferring her load to his desk and taking her in his arms. "As a soon-to-be college grad with a solid Beacon Hill bank account, you don't have to wear my hand-me-downs."

"I've discovered that that's one of the nice things about being rich," she said. "I can wear whatever I want."

"And the devil with Boston society?"

Carrie glanced around conspiratorially. "Haven't you heard?" she said in a stage whisper. "According to the Beacon Hill grapevine, I'm planning to turn the Carmichael mansion into a nonprofit boarding school for inner city kids."

Ben winked. "I wouldn't put it past you."

The mansion already served as home base for Partners in Promise, Carrie's new nonprofit small-business investment foundation, funded with every penny of her inheritance.

"Besides," she stepped back and plucked at the T-shirt, "I'm husbanding my money, trying to keep down overhead."

"Why don't you let me do the husbanding?" Ben reached for her again, but she danced past him to the desk.

"One more week, counselor." She waved a finger at him. "Believe me, I'm just as eager as you are to leap through that little loophole you discovered."

Smiling, Ben hiked a leg onto a corner of the desk. When it had finally come right down to the crunch,

Carrie had reconciled herself with her past. That hadn't come easily.

First they had a long talk, several long talks actually, mostly along beaches in Jamaica. Ben had taken her for another ride in Gordon Darnell's aged glass-bottom boat. They had sipped frosty drinks from Winston Brown's concessions stand. More than once while driving along the highway, they had passed Lester Darnell pedaling along on his new bike, a big box of aloe vera leaves balanced on the handlebars.

Later, Ben had decided that seeing young Lester hard at work was what had finally changed Carrie's mind.

At long last, she had bitten a large bullet and agreed to accept the inheritance—along with the Carmichael name—not for her own benefit, but for the sake of others. Lots of others, from the looks of all the case folders piling up on Ben's desk.

And that was even before it had occurred to Ben that Price Carmichael had made one big mistake. In his will, the old man had neglected to make a provision for Carrie to retain the Carmichael name in the event that she married. A week from tomorrow, they would step through that yawning loophole when Ben's beloved Miss Carmichael became Caroline Washburn Ross.

Carrie wandered to the window and gazed out at the expansive view. After awhile, she said quietly, "Uncle Price would have a fit if he knew what I have planned for the family fortune."

"Oh, I don't know." Ben joined her at the window and wrapped his arms around her. They both watched a gull glide past the window. "I have a feeling that, in his own way, Price would be very proud of you."

She tipped her head back to look up at him. "What on earth makes you think that?"

"Because you're his flesh and blood . . . and you're winning."

"But if I'm winning, he's losing."

Ben shook his head. "He's out of the game."

"Since when?"

"Since you forgave him."

"What makes you so sure I have?"

"Because I know you." He snuggled her deeper into his arms and rested his chin on the top of her head. "If you hadn't forgiven him, you never would have agreed to take his name. Not even temporarily."

She stood very still for a moment, then turned, settling her cheek against his chest. "Smarty pants."

He grinned. "I try."

Carrie feather-punched him in the chest, and leaned over to the desk to pull a tabloid-size newspaper from one of the thick accordion folders. "Look what came in the mail from Trish this morning." She unfolded the paper and held it up.

Ben found himself staring at a headline in a recent edition of the *Jamaica Daily News*.

RESORT BURGLAR LOSES APPEAL

"You don't say." He snatched the paper from her and

took his time reading the first few paragraphs. "Looks like good old Cousin Mark will be a guest of the Jamaican penal system until after our second-born arrives."

"Mark is not my blood cousin," Carrie pointed out for the umpteenth time.

"A mere technicality."

"And we haven't even discussed the ifs-and-whens of our *first*-born yet, dear." She snapped a finger against the paper to get him to put it down. "These things should be planned, you know."

He grinned again. "I can see I'm going to have to rescue you."

"From what?"

"From becoming a slave to efficiency." He planted a hand on the desk and leaned over to kiss her, keeping it soft and gentle, like a promise.

The kiss left her flushed and breathless. Stifling a chuckle, Ben stroked the side of her face with the back of one finger. He was having the time of his life, being in love with this woman.

Carrie cleared her throat. In a sudden flurry of action, she picked up a thick folder and handed it to him. "Lana sent a dozen more applicants."

He groaned, partly because he wanted to kiss her again, and partly because Partners in Promise was picking up steam so fast. "I haven't even plowed through all the other applications yet."

"Maybe you should take a course in speed reading."

"Maybe we should put a cork in the pipeline," he suggested.

"Never."

Ben fanned through the contents of the latest folder. Carrie had recruited Lana Fuller to keep an eye out for struggling entrepreneurs who might be deserving of startup financing from Partners in Promise. Apparently, Lana was taking the request seriously. Applications were flooding in from every location that Galaxy Tours visited.

"If Lana keeps this up, you're going to have to hire her fulltime," he said, then realized from the gleam in Carrie's eye that she had already thought of that.

"Well . . ." she said, "if Dexter Wilde doesn't scoop her up first. He already has her sending his foundation applicants for college scholarships."

"Let me guess." Ben pressed a thumb and two fingers to his forehead, as if conjuring images out of thin air. "By any chance, do I see Lester Darnell's name on one of those applications?"

Carrie bit her lip. "Lester's too young for college. But there's an exclusive boarding school in California that—"

"Say no more. I get the picture." He reached out and tweaked her nose, then kissed her again, long and deep.

"Edna might walk in and catch us," Carrie said, coming up for air.

"She must be getting used to that by now."

Calypso Wind 231

Carrie backed away from him, her face still flushed, her expression suddenly impish. "I came bearing wondrous gifts."

"I noticed."

She handed him the smaller of the two wrapped parcels. It felt heavy. Ben gave her a quizzical look. She bounced on her toes as he tore off the ribbon and paper. Inside, he found a brass-and-walnut plaque with the name of her new foundation engraved across the top.

"Partners in Promise," she read aloud. "Jonathan Benjamin Ross, Chief Legal Consultant."

He ran a fingertip across the etched lettering and whistled under his breath. "Incredible. I'm so impressed with myself."

She laughed. "You'd better be. I am."

Reaching for the second package, Carrie spotted the file folder that lay open atop the desk blotter. Tilting her head, she scanned the top page. Ben watched her eyes widen as she spotted the word *approved* scrawled on a corner of the application.

"Winston Brown?" She looked at him, eyes shining. "Winston is going to be our first client?"

"Make that Winston Brown and Associates. He and the Darnell brothers are joining forces in a limited partnership. I think they might have found a profitable niche with Winston's plan for an import co-op. They'll probably be able to open their New York store sometime next year."

Carrie fingered the second gift-wrapped package. "Then in a way, I guess, this makes me their very first customer. Gordon Darnell helped me order this."

She handed the package to him, then helped remove the wrapping. Ben held the box while she lifted off the lid and folded back two layers of cream-colored tissue paper. A familiar scent wafted from the contents. Brushing aside tiny bags of potpourri, she lifted out a set of white pillowcases bearing a richly-embroidered border of butterflies and tropical flowers.

"Custom-made by the Butterfly Lady," she said, fingering the intricate stitching. "So we'll always remember the island."

"As if we could ever forget."

Ben touched the colorful flowers, then Carrie's petal-soft lips. Her eyes sparkled. He took a deep breath, and when he let it out, he felt more content than he had ever been in his life.

"I love you, Carrie."

"I know. And that, dear heart, makes me the richest woman in the world."